FINDING LOVE
IN PAYTON

FINDING LOVE IN PAYTON

•

Shelley Galloway

AVALON BOOKS
NEW YORK

PRINTED IN THE UNITED STATES OF AMERICA
ON ACID-FREE PAPER
BY HADDON CRAFTSMEN, BLOOMSBURG, PENNSYLVANIA

To Gary and Cheryl, because they know all about dream houses.
To Tom, just because.
And to Mira Park, my editor, because she helped me realize I had a better book inside of me. Thanks!

Chapter One

"And don't forget the bananas," Daphne Reece called out to Jeremy as he headed out to the market.

"I won't, Mom," he replied, edging toward the door.

She continued. "Don't get the ones with nasty black bruises, or the ones that are pure green. Get bananas that look like they just turned yellow."

"Just turned yellow. Got it," Jeremy replied, biting his tongue from saying anything else. After all, getting directions in minute detail from his mom had been happening for as long as he could remember. Yet one more thing that came with being the youngest of five children.

Even if he was twenty-three years old and a college graduate. Even if he stood six inches taller than his mom.

1

"Now, about the steaks—"

He couldn't take any more. "Mom, I can pick out steaks. And I have your list right here." He smiled reassuringly, waving the list in the air for good measure. "I'll take care of it."

She still looked uncertain. "Do you want to go over the type of bread we'll need one more time?"

Please Lord, no. "I don't think so. I've gotten you bread before," he said dryly. Then, knowing more was worrying her than perfect ingredients, he sat down on the stool next to her. When she looked up, he curved his head down to meet her gaze. "Why are you so worried about this party, anyway? It's just family."

"I know, but it's Missy's birthday, too."

He hid a smile. Missy had now been married to his eldest brother Kevin for almost two years. And if he knew anything, it was that his brother doted on Missynlike the sun rose and set on her. Missy didn't have a thing to worry about, as far as receiving attention. She was no doubt already having a great birthday.

"Kevin will make it special, Mom. Shoot, I bet he's already delivered a dozen roses to her at work."

She smiled at the notion. "I bet he has . . . but that doesn't mean anything. She needs something special from us. A special party."

He glanced at the countertops. Each inch of space was filled with bags from Kenwood Mall or card stores. Interspersed with the paper shopping bags were about twenty ingredients for a cake. As usual, his mother had taken a good idea and run with it.

"Missy's going to be so happy about the party. She'll think it's real special."

Glancing at the countertops, her face finally softened. "I bet she will. She's just had so many knocks in life, Jeremy. And I know she doesn't have any family here. I just want her to feel part of the Reece family, too."

Impulsively, he took his mom's hand. "She will, Mom. I bet she already does. We have a great family."

Her lips curved. "We do, don't we?"

Oh yes, they did. The Reece family had lived in Payton, Ohio for generations, and were nothing if not a cohesive group. They did things together, supported each other, and so far had married off three of his siblings with enough fanfare for visiting royalty.

Over the years while he'd been at college, most of his siblings had found their way into adulthood. Cameron became a small town lawyer; his sister Joanne, the director of the Payton historical society and museum. Kevin, his eldest brother, had always been successful, but when he met Missy, he'd begun to actually take time to enjoy life. His sister Denise was off in California, doing her own thing, and he'd just finished his master's program in education and had accepted a teaching position at Payton High.

His parents meddled and played golf, arranged parties, and *cared*.

They were all doing just fine. And he would too, if he could just survive the summer. He'd decided to live at home, work at the country club, and save up some money until he found an old house he loved and wanted to buy.

Things would be great if his family would ever think about seeing him as anything other than a kid. He seemed to be perpetually seventeen in their eyes.

He stood up and took the list before his mother could add anything else and grabbed his car keys. "I'll be back in a little while, Mom."

"All right. Be careful."

"I will," he said as patiently as he could before stepping out to his car, a spiffy late model convertible RX7. He'd bought it after working two summers waiting tables and felt justifiably proud of it. Some things in life were well worth saving every penny for.

The early June weather was brisk, and the foliage was glorious. As he drove the winding roads to the market, he passed a few houses for sale and mentally made a note to get on the internet later and check them out. It would be a good idea to have an idea of where he wanted to live sooner than later. There were only so many detailed grocery excursions he wanted to do.

Finally he arrived at the market, grabbed a cart and proceeded to make his way down the grocery list, stopping to say hi to several ladies who'd been friends with his mom forever.

Then he was stopped short by a pretty blond and a crying two year old in the cracker aisle.

His first instinct was to take his cart and run from the screaming toddler, but there was something about the calm way that the woman broke open a box of animal crackers that made him want to see what was going to happen next.

"Bry, come on now. You need to settle down. How about a camel?"

The boy stared at her and immediately reached for the cookie. "Cookie," he blurted, and was granted a sunny smile.

"That's right," she said, like he'd just uttered something profound. "Cookie. Now hang in there so we can get through the rest of our trip."

Jeremy was impressed. His sister Mary Beth had a girl almost the same age as the baby, so he knew first hand just how ornery a crying toddler could be. "Looks like that did the trick," he said to the blond, liking the way her hair kind of flipped up around her neck. It looked shiny and shimmery, like liquid gold.

Surprised, she glanced at him. "Oh, I'm sorry. Have you been trying to get by?" She motioned with her cart, like she was about to edge it over to the side of the aisle.

He stopped her, actually feeling that he was in no hurry to continue grocery shopping. "Not at all. I just couldn't help but notice that you're a real pro with a box of cookies."

She smiled brightly, revealing a pretty set of white teeth and an adorable dimple. "Some would say I shouldn't be bribing him at all . . . or that I should at least be using fruit."

"I'm no expert, but I think you did great."

She laughed. "Don't be too impressed, we still have to get through the rest of the store."

Suddenly going grocery shopping had a whole lot more appeal than it did five minutes ago. "I do, too. If you don't mind, I'll keep you company."

She glanced at his cart. "Are you sure? You look to be about done."

He waved his list, which was now a crumpled, scribbled-on mess. "I'm actually shopping for my mother. And she's got quite a list."

"You shop for her often?"

"Only lately. And only when she's hosting a party and is going a little crazy." Holding out his hand, he introduced himself. "I'm Jeremy Reece, by the way."

"Any relation to Jim and Daphne Reece?"

"My parents."

She smiled in recognition. "My parents know your parents from the country club. It's nice to meet you. I'm Dinah Cate."

"Pretty name."

She tilted her head and chuckled again. "Thanks. And this is Bryan Thomas Cate. He's twenty-two months and a terror."

Bryan was currently sucking on a cookie and looked

rather pleasant. Well, if you didn't mind the cookie crumbs and goo that dribbled down his chin. "He doesn't look too terrible at the moment."

"Believe me, he's already adopted the Terrible Two's in all of its glory."

Jeremy walked beside her as they pushed their carts, wondering why he was so drawn to Dinah. Yes, she was pretty, with cute hair and soft pink cheeks. Her brown eyes sparkled. And she did have a nice figure.

And no rings on her fingers.

But it still didn't explain his attraction. Could it be her demeanor? So calm, so inwardly happy?

She seemed so different from most of the girls he'd been dating. Girls who were high maintenance and almost obsessively busy. This Dinah looked completely at ease grocery shopping on a Friday morning; like there was something special about it.

All he knew was that suddenly he was feeling the same way, too. And wanted to know a whole lot more about her. "Do you work?" he asked.

"I do. I own Beagle's Books down on Third Avenue."

"That's new, isn't it?"

"About a year old. It's small, but I stock the best sellers, and a fairly good selection of mystery and romance books."

"It sounds terrific."

"It is for me. Bryan can go there with me sometimes, when my mom can't watch him. I play old big band songs. And my dog hangs out there, too. It's made my life nice."

It sounded nice. "And your husband? Does he like the place, too?" he asked, ruefully realizing he was being painfully obvious.

Her steps slowed. "He . . . passed away."

"I'm sorry." He felt like the biggest jerk imaginable, trying to make a play for a widow in the middle of the cereal aisle.

But she just bit her lip and sighed. "I am, too." She stared at him for a long minute, then added, "My husband died in a car accident right after Bryan was born. So, it's been a while."

He glanced at her again. At the way she kept a hand on her baby, as if she just liked touching him. At the quiet strength that seemed to emanate from her. He was more drawn to her than he had been to any other woman in years. "Hard, huh?"

"Oh yeah. I loved Neil. I loved him a lot." Her smile faltered. "At first, I just wanted to dig myself a hole, crawl in, and never get out. But babies have a way of not letting you do that."

"So you started your own business?"

"Yep. And learned about all kinds of things." She shrugged. "I still miss Neil, but I've learned that life moves on. And . . . I'm learning that it's okay if I move on with it. So, I'm okay." She glanced down toward her son again, brushed a finger against his cheek. "We're both okay."

Once again he felt a deep, fierce, pull toward her. Clearing his throat, he said, "I just finished school; I did a five year program at Ohio State, got my master's with my bachelor degree. I'm going to teach history at Payton High."

"Congratulations. I bet you'll be a great teacher."

"I hope so. I loved student teaching." Suddenly, he felt so young, so immature. His accomplishments sounded pretty run of the mill compared to hers. He wondered what else he could say.

Bryan fussed again, and Dinah gave Jeremy an apologetic smile. "I think we better move on. His minutes remaining in the cart are numbered."

The baby did look like he was about to let loose with a loud cry any second. "Okay." He turned to her, studied her features as closely as he could without looking like he was staring. "What did you say your store was called?"

"Beagle's Books."

"Maybe I'll stop by there sometime."

"I'd like that." Bryan wiggled some more. Dinah murmured to him, placed a kiss on his little forehead. "I better go. Nice to meet you," she said hurriedly, then was off down the aisle.

After another minute, she and her cart had turned the corner and were out of sight. Jeremy stood next to a display of Fruit Loops, struck dumb. Had he really just fallen for that woman? It sure seemed that way.

Mentally he replayed their conversation, tried to recall her facial expressions as she'd talked.

Had she been interested, too? Had her pretty brown eyes given him any hint of approval?

He couldn't be sure. All he did know was that he would be paying a visit to Beagle's Books in the very near future.

And getting the rest of his mother's groceries in short order.

Well, that had been interesting, Dinah thought as she unloaded Bryan from his car seat, using her extra hand to grab two grocery sacks. Had that Jeremy really been flirting with her?

It had been so long since anyone had that she couldn't be sure. After all, having a baby constantly by your side pretty much fended off any prospective admirers.

Bryan had fallen asleep in his car seat practically the minute she'd started the drive home, and now, as she carried him inside, his sweet little head lay against her shoulder in a manner of complete trust.

With one hand she unlocked her front door, set the sacks on her kitchen countertop, and then as quietly as possible, laid Bryan in his toddler bed. Thankfully, he only stretched his legs when he made contact with the cool cotton sheets. With any luck, she'd be able to bring in the rest of the groceries, unload them, and might even manage to sort her mail and have a cup of tea before he woke up.

Just thinking about having a moment to simply relax spurred her on to complete her tasks as quickly as possible. It wasn't that she didn't love being with Bryan, it was just that she loved sitting quietly for a few minutes every now and then, too.

Finally she was sorting through magazines and bills, putting each in a stack, sipping on a hot mug of Earl Grey tea, when Jeremy's image came to mind.

He had been so open, so adorable, that it had taken all her control to not look at him with longing. She figured he was probably used to such reactions, anyway. Men with bronzed skin, blond hair, and piercing gray-blue eyes most likely had garnered such reactions as hers on an hourly basis.

But there had been something about the way he'd looked at her, like she was special; something about the way he'd pushed his cart next to hers down those few aisles that made her feel tingly all over. And then embarrassed.

He was at least a few years younger than her. He was just out of college, for goodness' sake! He probably saw her as some kind of weird mother figure.

She sipped her tea, pausing to reminisce. But he hadn't really seemed that way, had he? And the way his voice had softened when he said he'd stop by Beagle's Books hadn't seemed fake at all.

Dinah tried to recall if she'd had those same feelings with Neil, but she couldn't remember. Neil had been terribly handsome, but always larger than life and more than a little childish. He'd lived for each day as if it had been his last while she had worried about their future.

Perhaps it was inevitable that he would get into an accident by driving too fast at night while she was at home—nursing their new baby.

No, that wasn't fair, she chided herself. She'd loved him. She'd loved his sense of adventure, his spontaneity. She'd loved how he would bring her flowers for no reason and give her backrubs for hours.

But she'd also learned that his sense of adventure and spontaneity could also be a detriment. He'd forget doctor's appointments or dinner dates. He'd buy something cool for his car but forget about the electric bill.

They'd learned to make do, but it had been difficult at times. He'd done what he wanted and she'd done what had to be done.

But then one day he was gone, and she was still there, holding on to what was left of her life. Alone. The emptiness of it all still made her ache.

"Ma-ma-ma-ma-ma," Bryan called out.

With a sigh, Dinah set down her cup and hurried to his room. Thankfully she'd had twenty whole minutes to herself. More than enough to feel recharged.

"Hey, Bry," she said, pulling him into her arms and inhaling his sweet baby scent. "Up already?"

"Ma-ma-ma-ma."

"That's right. I'm your mama. And I love you," she said. "Ready for some dinner?"

He smiled broadly, reached out and grabbed hold of her shirt.

"How does chicken sound?"

"Ma-ma-ma-ma."

She laughed. "I guess it sounds just fine, huh?" And promptly put all thoughts of any other man, even blond, blue-eyed ones, out of her head.

Chapter Two

"Happy Birthday, Missy," Jeremy said, kissing his sister-in-law on her cheek.

"Thanks," she said, almost glowing with delight. "I'm so glad you're back from school."

"Me, too," he replied, thinking once again that Missy was the best thing that had ever happened to his brother. Kevin had hardly moved more than a foot from his wife the whole time they'd been at his parents'. In fact, he looked almost glowing himself. Something was up with the two of them.

His mother seemed to think the same thing, because she had hardly taken her eyes off her eldest son and his wife during the last hour. "More cake?"

"No thanks, Mom," Kevin said.

"You sure? I'll get it for you."

"Positive."

"I'll have some," his sister Joanne said.

"It's in the kitchen, dear," their mom said with a wave of her hand.

Joanne stood up and shared a look of bemusement with Jeremy. "Guess I can see where I stand around here."

Jeremy stood up as well, following her into the kitchen. "It's not your birthday, Jo," he said, just to get a rise out of her.

Playfully she stuck out her tongue. "Hush, little brother, or I'll tell Mom you've been talking about living here until Christmas."

Just the thought of that set his teeth on edge. "You wouldn't dare."

Grinning, she teased, "Tell me something good and I won't."

That was Joanne. Always full of mischief and games. His eldest sister was red-headed, terribly smart, and terribly accident-prone. Her husband Stratton, a physician, seemed tailor-made for her. Her outgoing nature complemented his reserve to a tee.

But at the moment, Jeremy had another woman on his mind, one he couldn't seem to ignore from the first moment he saw her. "I met someone today."

Interest sparked in her eyes. "Who?"

"Dinah Cate." He paused for a moment, trying not to sound too eager. "Do you know her?"

She tilted her head to one side, her long braid

swinging with the motion. "I do," she said, her voice tinged with surprise. "Her last name used to be Ryan. I went to school with her."

"And?"

"She's got a baby, Jeremy."

"I know that."

Her lips pursed. "She's great. Owns a bookstore."

"Ever been there?"

"More than once. Dinah's a friend."

Her reticence set his teeth on edge. "Well? What do you know about her?"

Joanne fussed with some dishes in the sink. She placed a few in the dishwasher before turning to him again. "Why are you so curious about her?"

He handed her a glass to stack in, now curious about why she was so hesitant to give him any information on the woman. "I don't know. I guess because there's something about her I find attractive."

"She's quite a bit older than you. Five years."

"Just like you are?"

Her cheeks pinkened. "I guess I sound ridiculous, huh?" Joanne glanced back towards the party; the rest of their family was laughing about something Cameron said and passing around Mary Beth and Cameron's new baby.

"A little," he agreed, though he had to admit the difference in ages did bother him a bit.

Jeremy watched her actions with more than a little bemusement. "I like her," she finally said. "She was never one of my best friends, but I hung out with her a lot when we were younger. Her husband was Neil Cate. He was very popular, great. Kind of a daredevil, always willing to do something for a dare or a laugh. Dinah and Neil were a great couple." Her expression sobered. "Neil died about two years ago in a car accident."

"That had to be hard on her."

Joanne nodded. "I think so. But . . . she got through it okay. Her mother's a doll, Mom knows her real well. And her dad hangs out at the club a lot. She sews really well. I've asked her to do some things for the museum now and then . . ." Her voice drifted off, and Jeremy waited for her to finish her thought. "Don't get me wrong, but don't you think you should be looking at someone else?"

"Looking at someone else? Like who?" Cameron said as he entered the kitchen.

Both Jeremy and Joanne groaned at the intrusion. Cameron was second oldest in the family, and while not quite as uptight as Kevin could be, certainly not afraid to tell either Jeremy or Joanne what he thought about things.

And Joanne didn't seem to have any problem including him in the conversation. "Jeremy is interested in Dinah Cate."

"Really?"

Jeremy bridled at his brother's bemused expression. "I'm not interested in her. I met her at the grocery store."

"You seem awfully interested in her, asking lots of questions and such," Joanne pointed out.

"What kind of questions?" Cameron asked on his way to the remains of the birthday cake.

"I wasn't asking a lot of questions," Jeremy said, picking up a plate as well. "We were just talking."

"I like Dinah," Cameron stated, looking at Jeremy directly. "Always have. She's got a level head and a pretty smile."

Joanne rolled her eyes. "Cam, like that means anything."

Cameron laughed. "It does. She's been through a lot. Got a lot of responsibilities, too," he said before eyeing his little brother with some concern. "Look, if you need a date, I think Mary Beth knows a few girls just out of college who are going to teach at her school. Do you want me to see if she can set you up with one of them? She said they're real cute."

"No." Jeremy couldn't believe he was even having this conversation with his siblings. He couldn't believe they were telling him he was too young to be interested in Dinah. Like he couldn't deal with a grown woman's responsibilities. "Forget I ever said anything."

"You still going over to the country club tomorrow?"

"I am," Jeremy answered. "Payton said he'd hire me for the summer, waiting tables in the restaurant."

"I heard he just hired a fancy new chef from Houston, Texas."

"Can't wait to meet her."

"Jeremy, can you stop by the museum later on this week?" Joanne asked, finally slicing a monster piece of cake.

"Why?"

"I've got a favor to ask you."

Immediately he felt a band of suspicion wind through his stomach. "Such as?"

She swallowed. "Civil War reenactment."

Jeremy looked at his brother in alarm, though Cameron was already sporting a deer-in-the-headlights look. "Pardon me?"

"We're going to do a march through town, and some people are coming in who want to take some pictures for a book or something that they're doing. I'm going to need all the men I can get."

Somewhere in there was an insult. He was sure of it. "Thanks. I guess."

"Cam's already promised he'd be there."

Cam's fork stilled mid-air. "I said I'd try, Jo."

"And Kevin? Dad?"

She looked away. "I don't know about them. They're both awfully busy."

"But I'm not?"

"School doesn't start for three months. Come on Jeremy, I'm going to need you."

"I don't know."

She winked. "I'll help you with Dinah."

"Help me? You just practically made it sound like she was old enough to be my baby-sitter."

"I won't do that anymore. I'll help you get a date with her."

"I can get my own dates."

"I'll put in a good word for you."

He raised an eyebrow. Joanne and practiced speeches didn't necessarily go together real well.

"I'll . . . I'll get Stratton to. Everyone listens to what he says."

That had credence. Everyone did listen to Stratton, and he was a great guy. "I'll stop by this week. After I get my schedule from Payton. Hey, you want me to tell him hi for you?" he asked, unable to resist teasing her about her ex-boyfriend.

"Please do," she said sweetly.

"We better get on back," Cameron interrupted. "Missy's about to open her gifts."

And with that, Jeremy followed his brother and sister, almost jealous of their happiness and stability. And, for once, their age.

Chapter Three

As the June sun poured through the front window, Dinah finally took a break from her paperwork and paused to enjoy the early morning sunshine. She loved early summer in Payton. It wasn't too hot yet, the trees and bushes still sported dozens of blooms, and the days were long enough to feel like she had time to spare after work.

June was also great because Valerie, her sometime baby-sitter, was home from college and could help with Bryan four days a week. Her mom enjoyed him, she knew, but Valerie's presence made everyone feel like there was a little more time in the day, and Bryan absolutely adored her.

"We're off to the park, Dinah," Valerie said cheerfully as she picked up Bryan's bag of tricks. "Then home to a bath and a nap."

"Great. I'll be home around six," she said, glancing up from a stack of catalogs.

"Take your time."

Dinah knew that neither would miss her, which made her feel both relieved and amused at the same time.

But she'd have plenty of opportunity to wade through her stack of mail and invoices now. Absently, she petted Bonnie, the beagle the shop was named after, and worked for a solid hour before any customers arrived, then smiled happily when they came with a vengeance.

She poured coffee for them into oversized ceramic mugs, helped select books, and chatted with her customers about recipes and such as they made their purchases. Every once in a while Bonnie got up from her cedar filled dog bed to be petted.

She was just helping Mrs. McClusky put her books in one of her canvas bags when Joanne Sawyer came in.

"Hi there Mrs. Mac, Dinah," Joanne said with her usual breezy smile in place.

"Joanne," Mrs. Mac said. "I'm not due in to work for another hour."

"Yes, ma'am," Joanne said with a gleam in her eye. Dinah had to laugh; Mrs. Mac was a large woman with the disposition of a ornery goat. And she just happened to be Joanne's husband's receptionist at the doctor's office.

Rumor had it that the only person Mrs. Mac was nice to was Stratton Sawyer. "May I help you, Joanne?"

"Not yet. I just came to look around."

"All right," Dinah said, waving goodbye to Mrs. McClusky and concentrated on ringing up another woman's purchase. As soon as the room cleared, both she and Joanne gave a comical sigh of relief.

"Would you like a cup of coffee?"

"I would, thanks," Joanne replied, already making her way to the back of the store.

Dinah followed. Joanne had come for a reason, but obviously she was going to get to her point in her own time. Dinah poured a generous amount of steaming coffee in a purple and orange mug with the words READ printed on the side, part of a gift from her mystery book club that met on Tuesday nights. As she handed the mug to Joanne, she sat down in the wide rocking chair next to Bryan's crib and waited.

She didn't have to wait long.

"I saw Jeremy yesterday. You know, my younger brother."

Dinah didn't miss the jibe. "I saw him yesterday, too. Well, I met him in aisle five at the grocery store."

"He told me."

Joanne's voice seemed to be both censorious and encouraging at the same time. Dinah continued. "Jeremy got to see Bryan in all his glory, having a hissy fit in the middle of the cereal aisle."

"I've been known to have those, too. Stratton's inordinately fond of bran cereal. My tastes have stayed near the kids' boxes."

Dinah laughed. "Anyway, we chatted for a little while. It's funny that I'd never met him before, since I've met the rest of your family."

"He's quite a bit younger than the rest of us."

Ah. "Well, he's a nice guy."

"He is. He just graduated from college, you know."

She knew. Dinah glanced at Joanne for a long moment. Was she actually warning him off of her brother? "He's going to be teaching at the high school, right?"

"Right."

"Ah."

Joanne sipped her coffee and eyed her over the brim. Dinah waited, still unsure if she was about to get hit with any more zingers. "We talked about you last night."

Dinah was glad she wasn't drinking any coffee herself, because she probably would have spilled it by now. "Is that right?"

"Yep. I told him about how we had been in the same class, how you had a baby . . ." Her voice drifted off.

"Well, I know you'll have a nice time being in the same town again. He spoke very highly of his family."

"He spoke very highly of you," Joanne blurted.

Dinah met her gaze. "He did?"

"He did." Joanne reddened. "I just thought you should know that."

"Thank you. I think. Um . . . is there a reason you thought I should know?"

"No. I'm just making conversation."

Dinah wasn't so sure. Joanne surely seemed to be on a search and rescue mission, and Dinah had the feeling that Jeremy was about to be rescued from her clutches. The idea didn't sit well with her, although she was sure Joanne felt justified.

Jeremy Reece had the perfect combination of blond movie star good looks and winsome wholesomeness that was hard to ignore. She wanted to stare at him and be his best friend all at the same time.

But he was young, and surely had no interest in someone like her . . . someone who had been married, had a child, and had been widowed all about the time he was getting his driver's license.

"Let me know if you need any help with the books," she said, hoping Joanne would end the conversation at that.

"I came about something else."

"Yes?"

"Sewing. Are you interested in a couple of projects?"

She usually was, as long as Joanne gave her enough time to do them. She made window treatments for a few customers, and had made a formal dress once for

Joanne. And she'd also made several gowns for a Civil War ball a year ago for some fundraiser for the historical society. Dinah enjoyed the projects; it made her feel good to have something so pretty to show for a few hours of hard work.

"I might be," she said. "What do you need?"

"One ball gown and two soldier uniforms, all Civil War era. We've got a reenactment of sorts for a benefit in August." Joanne looked at her hopefully. "I already have most of the material bought."

"When do you need them?"

"Not until August."

It was June 17. That was enough time. "I could do them, probably."

"If you could, that would be so great."

"Same price?"

"Yep."

The money would come in handy. And with Valerie helping her out, she'd probably even have the time. "I'll be happy to do the costumes."

"Oh, great," Joanne said, smiling. "I'll send someone by later with the patterns. You working until six?"

"Until almost six."

"Okay." With a happy sigh, Joanne set her coffee cup down and then ventured over to the book stacks. "Now I'm ready to shop. I need to get a couple of paperbacks for me and a new mystery for Priscilla Hayward. Have you met her yet?"

"Nope. Who is she?"

"She's Payton's new chef, and she's from Houston, Texas."

"And you're buying her gifts?" Dinah couldn't stop the surprise from her voice. After all, it was common knowledge that Payton Chase was Joanne's former fiancé.

"Just a new book. I heard she's super nice and kind of at loose ends. And a mystery lover. And . . . well, I figure she's going to need some friends since she has to deal with Payton all day."

Dinah burst out laughing. "Well, send her my way and I'll try and help her out."

Joanne smiled broadly. "I'll be happy to. Now I better get moving or Mrs. Mac isn't going to be the only one late for work."

Dinah chuckled and walked to the register, just as two gentlemen came in looking for the new bestsellers. It was sure to be a busy day.

Chapter Four

"Eveything is about the same. Dinner service begins at five, continues until nine. We'll offer a buffet on the weekends, a few daily specials, which you'll get to sample when you come in," Payton Chase said as he and Jeremy walked through the dining rooms of the country club.

They'd been touring and talking for over an hour, mostly chatting about college and fraternities . . . and about Priscilla Hayward.

"Have you met her yet?" Payton asked, looking a little awestruck.

"I haven't," Jeremy admitted, biting his lip in order not to smile. There was obviously something between Payton and his new chef, and he, for one, was smart enough to stay out of it. "If that will be all, I'll just go ahead and get my—"

Payton checked his watch. "She should be here by now. Let's go see her, shall we?"

Since Payton was already walking towards the kitchen, Jeremy simply followed him. Truth be told, it would be interesting to get to visit with the chef, if for no reason than to have the news before Joanne. After their conversation the night before, he was hoping to have news on anyone, anything before she did.

"Ah, Priscilla," Payton said. "Here's someone I'd like you to meet."

Jeremy glanced up and did everything he could to keep his expression simply polite and cordial. Priscilla Hayward was a looker. With long black hair that skimmed her shoulder blades, green eyes, and a tall, lithe build, she looked like she should be skimming the pages of *Vogue* magazine, not wearing a white apron and hanging out in a kitchen.

"Nice to meet you," he said, holding out a hand. "I'm one of the new waiters."

She looked confused. "Oh. Nice to meet you."

"Jeremy's a little more than that," Payton explained. "His family have been long-standing members of the club, in fact, his mother's on the board. Daphne Reece."

Recognition clicked into place. "Well, I guess we'll be seeing each other a lot, then."

"Jeremy's going to be Payton High's new history teacher. He's just here for the summer."

Jeremy waited a moment longer, sure Payton was going to tell her his shoe size and what annoying habits he'd had when he was twelve. But the manager was quiet now, seemingly content to just gaze at the chef.

He cleared his throat. "Um, are you enjoying our town? I heard you moved here from Texas."

She smiled, her lips wavering a little. "Yes, I think so. Things are really different here, but good. I'm living in a little house in the historic section of town." Looking apologetic, she said, "I have to admit, the country club is not quite what I had imagined."

Jeremy smiled at Payton, who looked like he was seriously reconsidering his idea of visiting with Priscilla. "How did you imagine it?"

Her eyes hardened. "Well, Payton here had told me it was quite a bit different than it is."

"Yeah?"

"Bigger. More . . . cosmopolitan."

Jeremy swallowed hard. Clenched his fist. Anything to not burst out laughing. "Cosmopolitan? *Payton, Ohio?*"

She reddened. Payton looked practically pained. "I had thought it was a little more . . . edgy. *Nouveau.* But now I'm finding that lasagna is still thought of as ethnic fare here."

It sounded like Priscilla had been told a couple of

tall tales. Jeremy felt bad for her; it was hard enough starting a new job without finding that all your expectations were off-kilter.

"What are you going to do?"

"Do?" Payton squeaked.

"Do?" Priscilla repeated. "Nothing yet. I'm just going to make what they ask me for a little bit . . . but look out for the specials!"

"I'll do my best to promote them," Jeremy said with a grin.

"Great! Before you know it, everyone's going to be craving goat cheese risotto and veal shanks."

Payton flashed his perfect teeth. "As long as we have Prime Rib on Fridays, everything should be just fine."

Jeremy wondered if the two of them even realized there was enough electricity between them to light a small town. "I think I'll get my uniform and head on out, then. I've got to stop by Joanne's place and pick up something from her."

At his sister's name, Payton's expression turned sober. "Tell her I said hi, would you?"

"I will. She said to tell you hi, as well."

"How's she doing? I haven't seen her lately."

"Fine. She and Stratton are doing just fine."

If anything, relief crossed his features. "See you tomorrow night."

"Will do," Jeremy said after shaking Priscilla's hand goodbye. "See you both tomorrow at four."

As he left, he couldn't help but chuckle. Payton and Priscilla were at it again, this time fencing words over an upcoming theme buffet.

And if he wasn't mistaken, he could have sworn he heard several board members' names on the planning committee. He shuddered at the thought. Priscilla was going to have her hands full on more than one front.

Cosmopolitan, indeed.

He wasn't chuckling when Joanne handed him a stack of material and three envelopes of patterns and commanded him to take them to Dinah Cate.

"Couldn't you do this yourself, Jo?" he asked, more than a little peeved. He wasn't ready to see Dinah again. And he really wasn't ready for his sister to send him places around town like he was her errand boy.

"Please, Jeremy? I'm swamped."

He glanced at her desk. As usual, piles of papers were strewn everywhere, calendars, pens, and an opened box of highlighters threatened to fall off the side of the table. "You're a mess, that's what you are."

Missy, who worked as her assistant, looked up from her own desk, which was neat as a pin. "She does know where everything is, I should probably add."

"I find that amazing, but not enough to run these over to Dinah." With sudden inspiration, he turned to Missy. "Isn't it about your lunch hour? You could drop these off."

Missy laughed. "Good try, but no. I've got two classes of second graders about to visit and I bring my lunch. You are the chosen one, brother-in-law."

"Jo . . ."

"No whining. Thanks so much," she said, hoisting the material into his arms. "Please tell Dinah thank you, and that I'll be calling her. And . . . I'll call you later this week and tell you when the first rehearsal for the reenactment will take place."

"I can't wait," he muttered as he filed out of the building, just as a school bus full of excited kids pulled up on the curb. He waved to a few of them and one of the teachers, then headed toward Beagle's Books, pretending that he wasn't excited to see Dinah Cate.

Did she dare act surprised when she looked up from her mystery and saw Jeremy Reece enter the shop, his arms full of navy blue wool and scarlet-colored silk? No way, Dinah decided as she got a good look at his expression.

It was full of resolution and brotherly irritation. She knew the look well, after all, she had two brothers of her own. "Hey, Jeremy," she said instead, standing up to relieve him of his burden. Bonnie approached also, and when he bent down to pet the dog, she gathered her wits.

"I thought you might be stopping by."

His eyes narrowed. "Did my sister tell you that?"

Big mistake. "No, but she was in the store earlier."

"And?"

Oops. "And, I had an idea, from where I don't know, that she might enlist your services. Since you're not working."

A muscle in his cheek clenched. "I start my job tomorrow."

Why was that a sore subject? "Well, then. I'm glad you had time today." She walked the fabric and envelopes to her back room, deftly depositing them in one of the many laundry baskets she used to cart books and Bryan's things back and forth from home. "Thanks for bringing this in."

"Where's Bryan?"

His question, and his presence caught her up short. How had he followed her to the back without her being aware of it? "He's home with Valerie. Valerie Redmond. Do you know her?"

"No."

"Well. She's home from college. This is the second summer in a row that she's worked as my nanny. He loves her."

Jeremy seemed to be in no hurry to step away from her. All at once she wondered if her hair was a mess. If her lipstick . . . had she even remembered to put any on today? Without the shopping carts between them, he looked bigger, his presence seeming to suck all the oxygen out of the room, leaving her breathless. "Well," she said.

"Well."

Frantically she tried to think of something to say. Anything to redirect her mind from thoughts about his broad shoulders; from his unusual gray-blue eyes, from the way she was happy to see him again.

Anything to remind her of Joanne's veiled hints that he was young. Much too young for her. "Um, well. Next time I see Valerie I'll have to tell her I met you. She's a nice girl, so friendly, and I don't think she's dating anyone at the moment."

"Are you?"

She stuffed her hands into the pockets of her apron. "No."

A hint of a smile played at the corners of his mouth. "I'm not either."

"We don't even know each other." The moment the words were out she tried to figure out how to get them back. Those were the wrong words to say. She was older than him! His sister was going to kill her if she even thought about dating him.

And Jeremy . . . surely he would want someone young. Someone without a baby. Someone without a marriage and another man's old coat in her closet.

The chimes at the front of the shop rang then and, hurriedly, she stepped forward. Jeremy moved to the side, just enough to let her get by, but not far enough to prevent their bodies from touching as she passed.

Just that brief contact made Dinah's pulse race. Jeremy Reece smelled good. Like starch and honey. And outside. "Do you run?" she asked.

"I bike. Why?"

"You smell . . . like outside."

"I was on the trail this morning. We ought to go there together sometime. We could take Bryan for a walk or something."

That did sound good, which of course made her nervous.

Not knowing what to say, she continued to the front of the store and exchanged pleasantries with the couple who had just entered. After offering them coffee, she stepped toward her counter, and slid behind it just as Jeremy approached. Anything to provide a barrier to her emotions.

"Thanks for bringing the material by, Jeremy."

"You're welcome."

She pasted a smile on her face. "Maybe I'll see you around."

His mouth thinned, and she could tell it was all he could do not to let out a torrent of words; he looked that frustrated. "I'll see you soon, Dinah. Take care."

"You too."

"And tell Bryan hey for me."

She laughed at that. "I will."

And then he left, leaving a longing in her heart and the faint scent of pine in his wake.

Chapter Five

"How was your day?" Valerie asked Dinah two days later as she walked in the living room and collapsed into her favorite overstuffed chair.

"Exhausting. I didn't think the UPS man was ever going to stop unloading boxes of books. Then I had to un-box them and enter everything into the computer. And Mrs. Edwards came in."

Valerie frowned at the last part. "How was she today?"

Dinah smiled. "Not too bad. She only stayed for an hour today."

"I don't know how you handle that. She's there sometimes two and three times a week and never buys a thing."

"I like her. It's just sometimes I don't get a lot of

work done when she's around." She had, though, she thought with a secret smile. And she'd even decided to close up shop a little early, at 4:30, just to get a chance to enjoy a Friday night for a change.

She had actually gotten a lot done today, and that made her proud. She'd have something to be happy about tonight when she went to bed, she realized with some pleasure.

When she was growing up, her father would sit with her at the end of each day and asked what she had done. Any accomplishment, playing with a friend, drawing a pretty picture, cleaning out a desk drawer, was met with praise. Sitting around doing nothing was not.

It was all she could do on some days just to relax.

Of course, Bryan's appearance in her life changed all that. Now each day was loaded with dozens of mini-accomplishments. It had been a long time since she'd sat down for any length of time. "Where's Bry?"

"On the living room floor, sound asleep. He was playing with the plastic containers, stubbornly saying, 'not tired, not tired,' then practically collapsed on them. Don't worry, it's only been about thirty minutes."

"Good, he'll sleep well tonight, then." Dinah stood up and reached for her purse. "Let me pay you, swee-tie, then you can run off and have fun. What do you have planned for this evening?"

Valerie's eyes lit up. "I've got a date."

"Oh yeah? Anyone special?"

"Maybe."

Dinah couldn't help but laugh. "They're all maybes huh?"

"Not this one. He's kind of special. And we've gone out before, so we're practically a couple."

Dinah couldn't help it, she did laugh at that. "I remember those days."

"Was it like that with you and your husband?"

Dinah sighed, thinking back. "You know, I guess it was. One day we were just dating, then somehow, we were a couple."

"Then you were engaged and married."

"Yep," she agreed, thinking that it all had gone by much too fast. "I hope you have a great time. And thanks for watching Bryan."

"No problem, Dinah. See you on Monday."

Dinah waved her off, then slipped off her shoes and closed her eyes for a long minute. It did feel good to do nothing! She'd have to tell her dad that one day.

As if on cue, the phone rang. It was her mother. "Want to go to the club tonight?" she asked after the usual pleasantries were over.

Dinah didn't go out much, but since it was Friday night and she and Bryan were just sitting home alone, the offer sounded pretty good. "You know, I think we would like that."

"Great. Want Dad and me to pick you up or to meet you there?"

"I'll meet you there." She checked the grandfather clock on the far wall. "It'll have to be early, though. Bryan will have a fit if he has to be good at seven P.M."

"So will your dad," her mom joked. "How about we meet there at six? That way we can eat before the crowd filters in."

Dinah didn't go to the Payton Country Club a lot with her mom, but the times she had the restaurant could have never been called crowded. "You think it will be busy?"

"Without a doubt. That new chef there is all anyone's been talking about."

"Have you tried anything yet?"

"No, but Mrs. McKinley has and she said the spinach chicken wraps are just to die for."

It did sound good. "Bry's still asleep, but I should be able to get him up and going soon. Save me a spot."

They chatted for a few more minutes, then hung up, leaving Dinah to finally hop off her chair and check on Bryan. And as soon as she saw him, curled up around a set of measuring cups, her heart melted.

"Hey there, handsome," she said, lying down on the floor next to him and rubbing his back. "How's my best man?"

His little eyelids fluttered open. "Mama."

"Yep. I'm home and we're going out to eat with Nana and Pa."

Bryan's little smile widened, then he held out a

hand to hers. Dinah clasped it with pleasure. "I missed you today."

He smiled again, revealing six teeth, then immediately replaced it with a frown. "Val?"

"Val went home. It's just you and me, buddy, okay?"

He sat up. "Okay." And then with another sweet smile, he was off, arranging containers again.

Dinah knew without a doubt that she would rather be with Bryan than most any other person in the world, even though Valerie's date did sound like fun.

Jeremy knew without a doubt that Payton and Priscilla needed to come to some kind of agreement, soon, because their constant bickering was going to drive him crazy.

If Payton wasn't following Priscilla around, giving her well-meaning advice, he was talking her up to Jeremy.

Not that he'd ever given Payton any indication he wanted to know anything about his love life.

And to make matters worse, Priscilla actually seemed to like the guy. More than once, Jeremy caught her making calf's eyes at Payton when he wasn't looking. And she'd actually stuck up for him when the golf manager said something snarky about him, too.

It would have been amusing if he didn't have to be a part of it all.

Lucky for him, he didn't have to deal with the two

of them much at the moment, because the dining room was packed. Already they had turned over tables twice, and if they were lucky, a few might even get turned three times. People were flocking into the restaurant to get a glimpse of the pretty chef and to try out her daily specials. Jeremy did his part by sampling each and telling everyone that it all was delicious.

And it was. Ruefully, he realized he was going to have to start biking a few extra miles a day in order to keep up with the extra calories.

"Here you go, Jeremy. Three orders of sea bass and one chicken teriyaki for table eight."

"Thanks," he said to Priscilla, then hurried out to give the Andersons their order.

Inwardly, he smiled. There were actually quite a few advantages to waiting on people who had known him all his life, especially when they learned that he was working to save money for a house. The tips had been great, and most folks had given him a break while he got used to the ebb and flow of the room. Nobody yelled at him if he was slow taking their order or refilling their iced tea.

But he had to admit that each day had gone a little smoother, and by next week he would be feeling more at ease.

Well, he thought that until he wandered over to table twelve and almost lost his bearings.

Dinah Cate was there, with Bryan and two people who could only be her parents. She looked up and gave him a million dollar smile as he approached, her dimple in full glory. "Hi, Jeremy. I was hoping you were working tonight."

"Hi Dinah. Bryan." With manners that would have made his mom and dad proud, Jeremy turned to her parents. "Hi there. I'm Jeremy Reece. I met Dinah the other day at the store."

Her parents eyed him with interest. Her dad, a husky man with a balding head of hair, held out a hand. "Mark Ryan. Nice to meet you. Jeremy Reece, huh? Any relation to Jim or Cameron?"

"Jim's my dad; Cameron's one of my older brothers. There's a whole crew of us."

"Jim and Cam are good lawyers. Decent."

Jeremy got a kick out of that. "They are that," he said before turning to Mrs. Ryan. "Ma'am."

She held out a hand, as well. Jeremy would have expected her to look just like Dinah, but she didn't, not really. Her eyes were brown and Dinah had her cheek bones, but where Dinah's hair was golden blond, Mrs. Ryan's was a more auburn color. And she also looked to be a few inches taller than her daughter. *Interesting.*

Mrs. Ryan shook his hand and smiled brightly. "It's a pleasure. I'm Winnie." A dimple appeared. "I know your mom; we've been on a golf league together. We practically kidnapped Dinah tonight. She's not one for going out much."

He looked at Dinah to see what she thought of that,

but she only looked happy, like there wasn't a thing her parents could say that she would ever worry about. *Interesting*.

"Well, I'm glad you came out," he said. "Our new chef is terrific." He went into the specials, describing each dish in detail, then opened up his small notebook to get their drink orders.

"Just iced tea, Jeremy," Mrs. Ryan said. "For three. And some apple juice for Bryan."

"Gotcha," he said before walking away to take care of things.

For the next hour, he took orders, and did his best for the six tables in his area, keeping an eye out on the Ryan family all the while.

He liked watching them, noticing how easily Dinah got along with her parents. Just watching them together made him think of his own family, and their easy camaraderie. He knew a lot of people who did nothing but complain about their parents . . . who had uneasy relationships with them. It made him feel good to know Dinah wasn't one of those people.

After an hour went by and they finished their dessert, he brought over a carafe of decaf coffee for Mr. Ryan. "Refill, sir?"

"No thanks, Jeremy. If I have any more I'm going to float away."

"Ma'am?" he asked Mrs. Ryan.

She also shook her head, though she smiled up at him above Bryan's head. Bryan had moved from his high chair to Dinah's lap to Winnie's during the course of the meal, and Jeremy would bet money that Mr. Ryan was just biding his time until it was his turn.

"Dinah?"

"You know, I am going to take a little bit more. Promise it's decaf?"

"I promise," he said, gazing at her more closely. She had on a sundress and a pink sweater, making her look like any college coed in Columbus. Her hair was curled at the ends and kind of bounced when she nodded, and her brown eyes were lit up like Christmas.

"Great. I sure don't want to stay up all night."

"What do you have going tomorrow, honey?" her mother asked as Jeremy refilled cups.

Dinah shrugged. "Not too much. Mrs. Martin is opening for me tomorrow, so I'm not going to go in until one or two. I guess Bryan and I will sleep in and go for a walk or something."

Her dad looked from Jeremy to Dinah. "So you've got a whole Friday night with practically nothing to do."

"I wouldn't call eating dinner with you two nothing," she replied.

Her parents exchanged looks and then eyed Jeremy again. "You're too young to stay home every night. When do you get off work, Jeremy?"

There was no way he was going to pass this up. "In about an hour or so."

"Dinah, why don't you let us take Bryan home? You and Jeremy could have a little time together."

Dinah's face colored, and Jeremy felt like a fool. He'd been practically ogling at her all night long. Her parents probably thought there was way more between them than there was.

"Mom, just because we talked about—"

"We know all about you, son," Mr. Ryan interrupted with a small smile, completely ignoring his daughter. "We've been sharing stories with Dinah about your family and such. Sounds like the two of you have a whole lot in common."

"Like a free Friday evening." Winnie smiled angelically.

Dinah looked mortified. Jeremy's heart went out to her; he knew exactly how she was feeling. Just as there was plenty of love in his family, there was also plenty of meddling. Not all of it welcome. "I'm sorry," he said to her quietly. "I'll just see you later."

But then her hand was on his forearm. "No," she said, a funny little smile playing across her lips. "I don't want you to think we were talking about you. Or that you're trapped or anything . . . but if you want to do something later . . . I would love to."

She would love to. He swallowed hard. "I'm glad," he admitted. Then, deciding that anything more that came out of his mouth would be embarrassing, he turned away. "I'll go speak with Payton about leaving soon."

Jeremy couldn't help but grin as he asked Payton to leave a little early so he could be with Dinah.

Payton glanced over at table twelve and smiled a little himself. "Sure, Jeremy. You don't have to ask, anyway. I'm just glad you're working as much as you are."

"Thanks."

"Welcome." Payton glanced toward the kitchens again. "What do you think I should do about Priscilla?" he asked, revealing that his mind was on far more than diners in the restaurant.

"Do?"

"She hates me," he explained, a crease forming between his eyebrows. "I kind of lied to her about the country club so she'd work here, and now she's counting the days until her contract is up."

Jeremy pretty much figured telling Payton that lying to employees was not a good idea, so he went for a safer approach. "Did you tell her you were sorry?"

"Only about a dozen times."

What else could a guy do when saying sorry didn't work? Since he'd never gotten too involved with any of the girls he'd dated, the problem was a little foreign. Finally he remembered Missy's birthday. "Roses."

Payton looked at him in surprise. "Roses?"

"Girls like flowers," he said, recalling how excited Missy had been to get flowers from her husband. "Roses seem to go a long way to solving all problems."

Payton brushed a non-existent piece of fuzz from his suit. "You may have a point. In fact, I think I'm going to do that. See, I'm crazy about her. I have been from the moment I saw her." He glanced at the kitchen again. "Weird, huh?"

Jeremy had a feeling Payton wasn't the only one who was crazy. He thought about Dinah practically nonstop and they had even less in common than Payton and Priscilla. "No, not so much."

Payton tilted his head towards Dinah. "You serious about her?"

"I barely know her."

"By the look on your face, I'd venture to say that hardly matters." He chuckled. "Go punch out and have a good time."

"You sure?"

"Heck, yes. Someone needs to have a good night tonight. We both know it's not going to be me."

Jeremy didn't need to hear that twice. After agreeing to meet Dinah at the bar, he went to go change clothes and clean up.

All of a sudden, he had a date.

Chapter Six

Dinah rubbed her hands on her thighs and tried to look relaxed. It wasn't easy, though. She and Neil had dated in college for three years, and then had been married almost two when he died.

Add two years to that . . . and it had been a long time since she'd dated. She felt strange and conspicuous, and more than a little odd, especially since she had the uneasy feeling that Jeremy Reece had probably just had a date the night before.

Probably with someone who needed a fake ID to get a glass of wine, someone whose body was perfect, not faintly lined with stretch marks. Oh, she wasn't going to lie and pretend she wasn't attractive on some level. She worked out and walked, watched what she ate. She still looked pretty good for her age.

But that was just it . . . she looked pretty good for a woman a few years from thirty.

And Jeremy Reece, with his movie star looks and muscular physique, could still make high school girls weep with crushes. Oh, he was going to have a time teaching high school.

"Oh," she murmured to herself as he walked toward her, a smile on his lips, wearing a dark blue button down and jeans so faded they were almost white. There was really something about him that was just mesmerizing.

"I'm sorry," he said as soon as he sat down next to her. "Getting cleaned up took a little while longer than I expected."

"It's okay."

He leaned forward, searching her gaze, like he really did care. "You sure? Priscilla, the new chef, had a few questions about the club and the town, and she looked so desperate I couldn't just walk away."

Dinah was pretty sure he couldn't. Jeremy didn't look to be the kind of guy who walked away from anything. Ever. "I've been just fine," she said. "Just thinking how long it's been since I've sat in a bar."

He looked concerned. "Hey, I wasn't thinking. Do you want to go somewhere else?"

She placed her hand on his arm. "No. I'm fine."

His muscles clenched under her fingers, and at that moment, Dinah had a pretty good idea that Jeremy was just as nervous as she was.

He gazed at her again. "Would you like to go for a walk? It's pretty out, and a little quieter."

Dinah glanced around the bar. It was pretty quiet where they were, except for a group of older men around the TV and two couples smoking in the back corner. But just thinking about being with him, being completely alone with him, was an opportunity she couldn't bear to pass up. "Yes," she said, "I'd like that."

He looked pleased. "Great," he said, hopping down from the barstool. "Here, let me help you," he added, taking her elbow.

She felt a little tremor as he clasped her bare arm, and felt almost tingly when he kept his hand at her arm, guiding her through the country club. And then finally they were outside. Stars and fireflies dotted green around them, making the night seem almost magical. "Let's go this way," he said, letting his fingers run down her arm until their fingers joined.

She let him hold her hand, and couldn't believe that something so innocent could cause such a feeling of happiness. Valerie had been right. Having a date was something to be happy about.

They said nothing for several minutes. Dinah was content to just walk along the sidewalk toward a park at the edge of the golf course, feeling her hand encased in his.

"I'm glad we're doing this," Jeremy finally said. "I hope you didn't feel trapped."

Trapped? "I was going to say I bet you felt that way. My parents . . . I don't know what was going on with them. I guess they were excited to even think I was interested in a man again."

He turned to her. "And are you?"

She glanced at him through the corner of her eye. What could she say that wouldn't embarrass either him or her? Not much. "I guess I stated that wrong," she said with a soft chuckle, trying her best to sound like she walked with guys in the dark all the time. "What I meant to say is that I haven't dated anyone since Neil died."

His footsteps slowed. "Why not?"

Now there was a question she hadn't even dared to ask herself.

"I hadn't wanted to, for one," she told him honestly. "And . . . there was no one who interested me, for two. And three . . ."

His footsteps slowed. "And three?"

"Well, not a lot of men want to date a woman who has a two year old." She glanced at him then, trying to see what he thought of her words in the dim light. But only shadows played across his cheeks, shielding his thoughts from her gaze. "My days and nights are pretty packed, between work and Bryan. There have been moments I've looked pretty harried. Most men would like to date a woman who at least looks like she's put together."

They walked some more. "And then, there's the whole idea of accepting another man's child. A lot of men don't want to take that on, either," she said, then almost bit her tongue. What was she doing, trying to convince Jeremy to stay away from her?

Jeremy nodded. "I can understand that."

Her heart fell. "You can?"

"Sure. A lot of guys, and girls too, I guess, would want to meet someone and start their own families." He shrugged. "It's a natural feeling."

"I agree," she said, recalling just how many nights she and Neil had stayed up, thinking of names for Bryan. What would Neil have done if she'd already had a baby? Would he have pursued her as doggedly? She doubted it.

"I'm not one of them, though," Jeremy finally said.

His confession brought her to a halt. "Pardon me?"

He looked at the ground for a long moment, now that they weren't making any pretense of walking at all. "I said . . . although I can see the difficulties, I'm not one of those guys who would be bothered by a woman who already has a baby," he said slowly, as if each word was measured.

Their conversation suddenly seemed a lot more intimate than holding hands. "Really?"

"Really. It would be a pleasure . . . to get to date a woman who is already so mature."

Mature. That didn't sound good. Right up there with

matronly. Instantly thoughts of stretch marks appeared once again in her mind. "Is . . . is that how you think of me?" she whispered. "As a mature woman?"

He shook his head. "I can't even place how I think of you," he admitted with a flash of white teeth in the dim light. "Though I have to tell you that right this minute . . . the last way I'm thinking of you is as a mother."

Dinah knew in her heart that she and Jeremy hardly knew each other, that there were a thousand obstacles and reasons that prevented them from being together. But, there was a portion of her heart that didn't care. A part that only wanted to think of how good it felt to wear a flirty sundress and to have someone notice.

Her heart beat in *staccato* to think that an attractive, single, extremely available man would ever think of her in his own time. "How have you thought of me?" she asked again.

"That I'm lucky enough to be alone with you. That I hardly even know you . . . and that I'm dying to kiss you right here, in the middle of the golf course," he said with a wry smile.

Her lips formed a small 'O'.

He looked at the ground again. "Childish, huh? Here you are, wanting to have a real conversation, to talk about our feelings, and all I'm thinking is that your hand feels so good in mine, that your shoulders look so pretty and tan in that sundress, and that I'd bet money that your lips would feel like heaven." He chuckled. "I'm sorry."

He was sorry? For making her feel desirable? Speechless, Dinah fought for the correct words to tell him that he had nothing to be sorry about. How she would love to kiss him, too. How even though she had an adorable baby at home there was a whole lot more to her than being a mom.

He sighed, ran fingers through his hair and started walking again. The charged moment relaxed, making Dinah wonder if she'd only imagined the tension between the two of them. "I heard from my sister Denise today. Would you like to hear a story about her?" he asked, breaking the silence as they walked toward a street light.

"Sure," she said, clasping her hands in front of her in order to not feel so sad that he'd dropped her hand.

He smiled at her. "Well, we're pretty close, since she's only three years older than me. And she's always been something of a complainer."

"Is that right?"

"Oh, yeah. You name it, something is wrong with it."

She had to smile at his explanation. "She sounds tough to live with."

He chuckled. "She was . . . though she'd tell you she's merely a perfectionist, and that she works really hard to do things just right. Anyway, a few years ago, back when Kevin had just started working and Cameron, Joanne, and Denise were in high school, Denise brought home an injured squirrel."

Dinah's mind spun as she tried to keep track of all the names. Once again she tried to recall all five Reece siblings, in order. Kevin was the oldest, followed by Cameron, then Joanne, then Denise, and finally Jeremy. "An injured squirrel?"

"Yep. Poor little thing must have fallen from its nest, or been injured by an animal, or something. Anyway, it was the meanest little furry creature you can imagine."

"What did your parents say?"

"My dad talked about rabies and diseases, my mom tried to get Denise to keep it in the garage . . . and the rest of us gave her grief over the poor little thing. None of us saw it as anything but an ugly nuisance."

"That doesn't sound very nice."

"It wasn't. But the thing hissed and growled. And it was pretty ugly, too. And it kind of limped around." Jeremy gazed out into the empty greens before them before turning back to her. "But Denise couldn't stand it. She was sure it needed help. She called up the vet and asked if they'd look at it."

"And the vet said . . ."

"You bet." They walked some more, and Dinah couldn't remember ever having such a nice time. "Well, my mom refused to take the squirrel to the vet. She kept saying it was just going to die."

"I can't imagine your mother being so mean."

"You're right. She's a very nice lady . . . but she also was on a budget. Five kids, one in college, another one about to go . . . my mom had a pretty good idea that this squirrel on its last legs—literally—was going to cost us a week's worth of groceries. So Denise made Cameron take her."

Dinah had to laugh as she tried to imagine what her own older brother would have done. "Cam?"

"He just got his license, and Denise knew he'd stayed out thirty minutes past curfew the weekend before and wasn't afraid to blackmail him in order for him to say yes."

Dinah laughed. "So off they went."

"Yep. Cam driving, complaining all the way, Denise holding this very injured, terribly mean squirrel in a cardboard box. Joanne and I went along for the ride."

"What happened?"

"The vet said the squirrel was in a lot of pain, probably had some kind of internal bleeding, and gave it a shot to put it to sleep."

Dinah winced, imagining the whole crew of siblings supporting Jeremy's sister. "Oh. Poor Denise."

Jeremy nodded. "She started crying, right there in the vet's office. Talked about how it never really got a chance to have a good squirrel life." He waved a hand. "It was something out of a really bad soap opera."

Dinah chuckled. "What did the vet do?"

"He hugged her. Told her something about how she had done the right thing by taking care of it so it wouldn't suffer." He gazed out at a thicket of trees. "Cam took her out to ice cream, and the rest of us got a cone, too." He smiled softly. "It sounds horrible, but that was a great afternoon. It was the first time we were all part of an adventure without our parents. We went home that night, never saying a thing."

"Well, all of you were there except Kevin."

Jeremy shook his head. "Kevin never did any of that stuff. He was always too mature."

Dinah breathed deeply, enjoyed the aroma of cut grass, the sounds of crickets and bull frogs. She imagined Jeremy being so excited to be on a grand adventure with his older siblings. "So, did Denise ever tell your mom that Cameron took her to the vet?"

"Oh, yeah. We told Mom and Dad the whole gory story a few years later one night at dinner."

"What did your parents say?"

"My mom looked at Denise and squeezed her hand and said that that was what made her special. Some people were able to handle difficult situations while others liked to push them away. She said she admired Denise for doing something about the squirrel, even if the outcome wasn't what she had hoped for."

"What did the rest of you say to that?"

"Nothing. Cam had sworn us to secrecy and bribed us with ice cream," he said, with a fond smile. "Even two years later we knew better than to say much."

He laughed again at the memory. "I guess I told you that because you remind me of Denise in a lot of ways, Dinah."

She couldn't have been more surprised. "How?"

"You've taken on difficult situations, cried a little bit, and have done your best. You've started a business so you could spend time with Bryan, you've let people help you when you've needed it, and you don't complain." His voice lowered, the new pitch putting her nerves on end. "I think you're pretty incredible. Your accomplishments awe me, just like Denise's stubborn need to do something about a little animal that no one cared about awed me, too."

She didn't know what to say to that, though she was touched. "Thank you."

"You're welcome."

They came to the end of the path. The outline of the clubhouse stood bold in the distance, illuminated by a ring of ornate iron street lights. But darkness hung around them, blanketing them like a heavy cloak. "Would you like to go back inside for a cup of coffee or a drink?"

She would, but there were too many conflicting emotions brewing through her at the moment. Too many feelings burning inside her that she wasn't sure she was ready to discern and handle. "I'd better get on home," she said, though her feet didn't want to move. She was having such a good time, and was so attracted to Jeremy. It was really too bad she was feeling so confused about everything.

He squeezed her hand. "All right."

She tried to think of something else to talk about, anything that didn't involve her. "How's work?"

"It's fine. Good money."

"So, you're looking for a house?"

"Yep. I want an old one, like Cameron and Joanne live in. Some place with some history to it." He glanced at her. "Is yours like that?"

"Goodness, no. It's in a new subdivision, and has the same floor plan as at least a dozen other houses in the neighborhood." Then, because Neil had picked it out and she felt guilty for putting it down, she said, "I like it."

"Missy and Kevin have a new house, too. Missy teases us sometimes, says that old plumbing and electrical work is overrated. I'm drawn to the older places, though. And some of them are in my budget."

Their pace increased, and within minutes they stood by Jeremy's car. "Ready?" he asked, already opening the passenger-side door.

"Ready."

He helped her in, then walked to the driver's side. Dinah had a curious sense of *déjà vu*. It had been so long since a man had done that for her that she felt as if she was back in high school.

Jeremy pulled out of the parking lot, then switched gears as he drove down the almost empty street with the kind of satisfaction that only a man can get out of a well-built sports car. "I like your car."

"Thanks. It's old, too," he said with a chuckle. "This represents hours of waiting tables in Columbus."

"You do that, huh? Work hard to get exactly what you want?"

"I do," he said, after getting directions to her house. "I'm patient and hard working, and I don't mind waiting until I get exactly what I want."

An offer hung in the air, and Dinah could tell that Jeremy was certain she was worth waiting for.

Was she? She didn't know anymore. All she did know was that she couldn't risk kissing him until she knew how her feelings stood. After all, she couldn't just think of her future, it was Bryan's future as well.

When he pulled into her driveway, behind her parents' car, he turned to her. "I'm glad you stayed late and went for a walk with me."

"I am, too."

"I'm going to go look at houses on Sunday, but then I thought I'd go have some lunch on the bike trail. Would you and Bryan like to come?"

"I don't know."

"Oh."

She heard the disappointment in his voice and tried to explain. "I guess I'm not sure what my feelings are for you," she said before even weighing how her words might sound. "How I feel about dating you."

His body stiffened, as if her candor was disconcerting. "Is it my age?"

"Partly," she said honestly and with more than a bit of sadness. "But . . . it's also Bryan, memories of Neil, and the fact that I haven't done this before." She tried to think of words that could convey her doubts about herself, about her life, about her past, but none was available. It seemed as if her whole jumbled mess of emotions was stuck somewhere in the depths of her mind, twisting up her thoughts. "Please don't be mad."

"I'm not. I'm not, I promise." He stared at her hard, then shut his eyes before speaking. "I know you don't want me kissing you, but I've been dying to do this since the first moment I saw you," he said softly as he raised his right hand and slowly, as if with great thought, brushed it through her hair.

The tips of his fingers were slightly rough, and the coarseness reminded her once again just how attractive she found him.

Doing her best to keep the mood light, she chuckled. "You wanted to feel my hair?"

"Yeah. It's so shiny and golden." He rolled his eyes in the dim light. "Pretty stupid, huh?"

If he even knew how she was feeling at the moment Jeremy would say *she* was acting pretty stupid. Time to call it a night. "Well . . . I better go. If I know my parents, they're probably watching me out the front windows."

"All right. Dinah, let me know what you want to do about us . . . or if there is even an us."

"You'll leave it to me?"

"To you," he said. "Good night."

"Good night, Jeremy," she replied, as she made her way up the front walkway and into her house. Feeling suspiciously like she did after a date in high school, wanting to do nothing more than go to her room and replay every moment of her night.

But somehow she didn't think her parents, who were perched on the edge of her couch expectantly, would let her. Somehow she knew they'd keep her on the couch with them until they got a full report of her evening with Jeremy.

Chapter Seven

"**S**o what kind of house are you looking for, Jeremy?" Mary Beth asked as she, her mom, and he pulled out of his parents' driveway and began a house tour a week later.

He shrugged. "Something in the historic section of town, maybe with some woodwork. Couple of bedrooms."

Mary Beth scanned the MLS guide. "Number of bathrooms?"

"At least two."

"Garage?"

He knew better than to hope for much. "I'm hoping for at least a single car, or at least a covered carport."

She wrote that down. "Does it have to be attached?"

"Nope."

As Mary Beth flipped through a few more listings, circling a few with a yellow highlighter, she glanced at her mom. "What do you think?"

Marianne McKinley glanced over at her daughter's highlighted markings, then tapped at two with a long pink nail. "I've got a few ideas, and the ones you circled might appeal to Jeremy. Let's start there. Go ahead and start calling, hon."

Jeremy leaned back in the backseat and watched the two women work. "I didn't know you knew so much about real estate, Mary Beth."

"I don't." She smiled, her face full of good humor. "I mean, I don't know it like teaching kindergarten. But I know some from watching Mom all these years. And after my experience with the money pit house, I feel an obligation to all family members to help out."

Jeremy laughed. Mary Beth had bought a run-down home with more problems than the class of cute kindergarteners she taught. Thank goodness she had met Cameron soon after she moved in. He helped her fix up the house, and they fell in love soon after. "Thanks for helping me out."

"You're welcome! I'm glad to help. Plus, it's nice to let Cam have some time with Maggie."

"What do they have planned today?"

"I think he's probably going to run a few errands then go to your house." She rolled her eyes. "Cam will hang out with your dad, watch football, let your parents fuss over Maggie non-stop, then tell me that he is such a great dad."

"Isn't he?"

"Yes," Mary Beth laughed. "He is."

All that talk of babies made him think of Dinah and Bryan. "Has it been harder than you thought, juggling it all?"

Mary Beth shook her head. "No. I've really enjoyed it," she admitted. "But then again, I've had a lot of help. And although I give Cameron a hard time, he's never complained about changing diapers, or getting up in the middle of the night, or helping with the laundry. It would be pretty hard to do it by myself."

"Yeah, I guess so." Dinah's ease with Bryan flashed through his mind again. She made parenting look so easy, she was so patient. Did she ever have harried days?

Marianne stopped in front of a white clapboard home with an almost nonexistent front walkway. "This place needs some help in the front, but I heard the backyard is heavenly," she stated. "And it's empty, so we didn't have to wait to schedule a showing. Let's go take a look."

Jeremy wandered through the house after Marianne, listening to the pros and cons of the house with half an ear. He wasn't sure what he was expecting, but he knew he wasn't going to buy anything based on the dimensions of a specific room.

He knew he was looking for something that made him feel good, something that felt like home.

This one didn't.

He told Marianne so, and with a shrug she locked up the door and took him to another house.

And another. And four others after that. Some were already lived in, two others were vacant, and had been for some time.

"I'm sorry," he said as they walked down a stone walkway back to Marianne's car. "I don't know exactly what I'm looking for, but I know it's not one of these."

She looked surprised by his apology. "I didn't think you'd find a house today, Jeremy. I had a feeling that you want might take a little time. Good things always do." She turned to her daughter. "What do you want to do?"

Mary Beth scanned her MLS list one more time. "How about we go to this last house on Maple, then get a cup of coffee at the Mill and plan our next meeting?"

"Sounds good to me," Jeremy said.

Marianne glanced at the address again, then pulled away from the curb toward Maple. "Someone saw you out walking with Dinah Cate the other night," the older lady said as she weaved in and out of the light traffic.

"We were out walking," he said, wondering what it was going to lead up to. He glanced at Mary Beth quickly, but she didn't seem to be aware of where her mother was headed.

"I've always liked that girl. Do you know her, Mary?"

"A little bit. I actually knew her husband pretty well. We were in a few of the same classes in school."

"Which ones?"

"French. And a chemistry class, too, I think. Neil was a nice guy. Always had his eye on Dinah."

"I thought they didn't date until college?"

"I don't think they did. Dinah didn't date much in high school, and Neil was kind of wild, dated a lot of girls, kind of the more adventurous type. I think he just sort of watched Dinah from afar."

"It's too bad he passed away."

"Yes, it is. She had quite a time of it for a while there, raising that baby, dealing with lawyers and insurance people. Cameron actually handled a lot of the estate."

"I didn't know that."

"You know Cam . . . he'd never say a thing about it. That's why he's such a good lawyer."

Jeremy slumped back against the leather upholstery. "I guess so." He didn't know what to think, other than Dinah had a whole history that had played out while he was in college. Somehow that made their differences feel more marked.

He tried to recall if he had known her back when

she was still in high school, but he couldn't place her, beyond a pretty girl with a cute figure who was a friend of Joanne's. For the first time he wondered if maybe everyone else was right; maybe he was too young for her.

Perhaps she needed someone who had known her circle of friends, or Neil's, or had helped her during the time when she was putting herself together? Someone who saw her as a woman just off the brink of a difficult time in her life?

Not some guy who only saw her as adorable and accomplished.

"Now this place has possibilities," Marianne said, staring at the house in front of them.

Jeremy glanced out his window and whistled low. The place was unlike anything he had ever seen. It was stone, not wood, and had enough angles and turrets that it looked like someone's dream house gone wrong.

But it was attractive in its own way. The rich brown stones were aged and worn, giving the house a homey, rich feeling all its own. The roof looked to be in good repair, and the windows were arched and framed with quality wood, painted brown.

It sat on an oversized lot filled with trees, all types of trees, pear and maple, ash and pine. Each looked to be in good health, and surrounded the house like a picture frame.

"This looks like it's out of a fairy tale," Mary Beth said, in awe. "I can't believe I've never noticed it before."

"It's been in a gentleman's family for years and years," Marianne said, glancing at a pile of notes in her day planner. "If I'm not mistaken, this house has some history to it, as well. I think some people brewed moonshine in it during Prohibition."

Jeremy got out of car, immediately charmed. "Is it vacant now?"

Marianne McKinley nodded. "Yep. Mr. Burton decided to go live in a retirement community, and his nephew just cleaned it out and put it on the market last week. And, he cleared out about twenty trees," she added. "That's why you never noticed the place, Mary Beth. It used to be practically hidden from the road."

"I like the fence," Mary Beth said, pointing towards the split rail fence stained dark brown in the back yard. Years ago someone must have planted vines along it, because it was half covered with honeysuckle vines.

"I do too," Jeremy said.

Marianne unlocked the door and led them inside, and each oohed and ahhed over each meticulously kept room. The floors were wooden, the woodwork white. The only flaws were the seriously outdated kitchen and one bathroom.

But Jeremy knew he'd found his home. "How much is it going for?"

Marianne named the price. Jeremy stared at her in surprise. It was priced even more competitively than the others he'd seen. "Why so low?"

She shrugged. "I don't think the nephew wants anything to do with it. He's more of a tract house kind of guy."

"What do you think?" he asked Mary Beth.

"I love it," she stated, not even missing a beat. "I love how charming it is . . . and there's room to add a bath off of the back, as well as places to remodel the kitchen. But I wouldn't change a thing about the front of the place, Jeremy. It's just beautiful."

"It was built in 1910, and has been remodeled three times," Marianne said, then proceeded to go into detail about the dates of plumbing and electrical renovations.

But Jeremy wasn't listening; instead, his mind kept drifting to the pretty backyard, and how perfect it would be for a toddler to play in.

He thought of how nice the front room would be with wall-to-wall bookshelves and two overstuffed chairs, how the side street was within walking distance to downtown yet off the main streets.

"I like it, too," he said. "A lot."

They walked around a few minutes more, then drove to a coffee shop named the Payton Mill and sat in front of the large picture window. "It's got possibilities, Jeremy."

"It does. Do you think it's going to go fast?"

Marianne shrugged. "I hate to predict these things, but honestly . . . maybe."

Mary Beth laughed. "I guess it will all depend on how long you want to think about it. And how long you want to live at home," she said softly, with just enough edge that Jeremy had to laugh.

Like him, he knew Mary Beth loved her parents dearly . . . but would never want to live with them for any length of time.

"There is that," he said, mentally calculating how much money he'd managed to save over the passed two years. He'd made very good money waiting tables at an exclusive restaurant outside of Columbus, and even managed to add to it by working as a tutor while he was student teaching. It wasn't a large amount by anyone's standards . . . but it was just enough to pay the down payment on a very small home.

Jeremy was just about to try and figure out how much he could earn over the summer when he noticed Dinah walking up the sidewalk with Bryan. She had on crisp white shorts and a tan T-shirt, gold earrings in her ears, and black sunglasses. She looked slim and chic. Young and vibrant . . . anything but a toddler's mom. As she approached, she set Bryan on the ground and let him lumber in front of her.

And then finally they were in the Mill, as well.

"Look who's here," Marianne said with a smile. "Hey there, Bryan! I like your overalls."

"Say thank you," Dinah said to Bryan before smiling at Mrs. McKinley. "Hey there, Marianne. How are you?"

"I'm fine. Just sitting here with Mary Beth and Jeremy Reece . . . I believe you know each other?"

Jeremy watched as her easy smile became stilted, all in the time it took her to meet his gaze. "Hey."

"We've been house hunting. What are y'all up to today?"

"We've gone on a little bike ride, and now we're getting set to go to the store for a while."

"Won't you join us?"

Dinah glanced at Jeremy. "Are you sure?"

"Yes," he said, unable to do anything but stare at her.

Her cheeks turned rosy. "Well, then, let me just go order some drinks and I'll be right there."

"We'll take Bryan, Di," Mary Beth said, already scooping up the toddler and talking to him.

Jeremy's heart felt like he'd just run two miles. There were so many thoughts running through his head, he didn't know what to think. All he did know was that it was pretty uncomfortable sitting with Dinah and Bryan with his sister-in-law there. And Mrs. McKinley, who was friends with Dinah's mom and his.

No telling what was going to get back to his parents. Yeah, right. *Everything* was sure to get back to his parents!

"Jeremy," Marianne said, as if on cue.

"Yes?"

"I just want you to know that I think it's great that you and Dinah met each other. You both have such amicable personalities."

He glanced at her in surprise. For once, Marianne looked completely serious, earnest. "Each of you needs someone who's bright and sunny. Steady. You would do well together."

"You don't think the age difference matters?"

"Sure it does," she said with some surprise. "But doesn't everything? I've yet to come across a couple who have nothing to overcome. Y'all's differences just happen to be easy to spot."

He was prevented from saying anything by Dinah's approach. She held a cup of juice in one hand and a mug of steaming hot coffee in the other.

"Tell me about the houses," she said with a grin. To Marianne, she said, "Jeremy told me earlier that he was looking for a place with character."

"I'd dare say he found it," Mary Beth said, handing Bryan over to Dinah as she sat down. "Jeremy found the greatest place over on Maple." She went on to describe it, her mother adding details here and there.

Jeremy kept quiet, choosing to give his attention to Bryan. The little boy didn't seem to mind being stared at, at all. In fact, the boy seemed to like him just fine. He made a note to himself to bring Bryan a box of animal crackers next time he stopped by Dinah's bookstore.

He'd just held out his arms to Bryan when the

Mill's door opened and Joanne flew in. "Well, look who stopped by," he muttered. Now he knew for certain that everything that happened was going to get back to his parents . . . as a minute by minute replay.

Chapter Eight

If Joanne was taken aback at the sight of Jeremy holding Bryan, she didn't show it. As soon as she entered the coffee shop she waved to them, walked toward their table, and pulled up a chair after a round of hello's.

"You, my brother, are surrounded by women," she teased, reaching out to rub Bryan's ankle.

"Thank goodness for Bryan here, or I'd have to leave," he joked.

"Don't worry, Jeremy, if it wasn't for Bryan, we would have kicked you out long ago and ventured into girl talk," Mary Beth quipped before turning her attention to Joanne. "What's going on?"

"I just brought Stratton some lunch. He's working late today and couldn't leave," Joanne explained.

"And, I have quite a bit of work to do for the reenactment."

"I started the costumes yesterday," Dinah said. "I should have the first soldier's uniform ready for a fitting in about a week."

Joanne turned all business. "Great. Get with Jeremy to do that."

"Jeremy?"

"Me?"

Joanne glanced at the pair of them like she couldn't believe they could be so dense. "Well, yes. One of the costumes is for Jeremy. You'll be able to make sure he's all set, right?"

Jeremy caught Dinah's eye once again, and he could have sworn she blushed. "Sure," she said.

Joanne smiled.

Suddenly, being around Dinah, in the company of his sister and sister-in-law, and her mother, was more than he wanted to deal with. There was too much between him and Dinah that hadn't been resolved, the least of which was him asking her out and her telling him no.

With one last reassuring pat to Bryan, he stood up. "I'm going to go ahead and take off," he announced. "Thanks, Mrs. McKinley, for taking me around. You, too, Mary Beth."

All four women looked at him in surprise. "Are you sure you want to leave?"

"Oh, yeah," he said. "I think it's best."

"See you tomorrow at Mom and Dad's?" Joanne asked.

"Yep. I'll be there." Against his will, he glanced at Dinah. She was staring at him with soft brown eyes. Like she actually cared he was leaving.

Well, that was something, he guessed. "Let me know about the fitting, Dinah."

"I will," she said softly, reminding him of their walk in the dim light.

His collar felt tight and it wasn't even buttoned. It was really time to take off. "Bye," he said, then got out of the Mill as quickly as he could and walked away.

He walked through the parking lot, only to realize that he had no car. Grumbling, he wandered down the block toward the country club. Maybe he could put in a few extra hours and beg Priscilla or Payton to give him a ride home later.

Dinah watched him leave with a sinking sensation. He'd left because of her and she felt terrible about it. "I'm sorry," she said to the women around her who seemed perfectly content to look at her with amused expressions. "I didn't mean to cause a problem."

"You mean because Jeremy took off?" Joanne asked.

She shrugged. "Yes. I'm sure you love these chances to get together, as a family."

Joanne chuckled. "We get together often enough. I promise! Listen, if he left for any reason, it was because of me. I drive him crazy," she stated, not looking one bit perturbed about it.

Dinah knew she wouldn't forget Jeremy's wary expression around her anytime soon. "I don't think so."

"I bet it really is the number of women, Dinah," Marianne McKinley said kindly. "My goodness, there's practically enough of us to throw a slumber party! Any man would leave in a hurry." She leaned forward, the discussion settled. "Now, tell me, how was that walk of yours?"

Mary Beth winced. "Mother, Dinah doesn't need to share her personal business with us."

"She doesn't mind," Marianne retorted. "You don't mind, do you?"

"I don't mind. There's really not much to share," Dinah admitted, wondering why that made her so depressed.

"And you don't have to tell us anything," Mary Beth said, glaring at her mother. "Although . . . I've always wondered if Jeremy kisses as dreamily as he looks."

Joanne frowned. "Ew. That's my brother we're talking about."

"Your brother is a dreamboat," Mary Beth laughed.

"You're married to his brother."

"Who's my personal dreamboat," Mary Beth said with a smile. "I don't want to kiss Jeremy, I just wanted to know if my hunches were correct." She glanced at Dinah and smiled encouragingly.

Dinah squirmed. "I don't know," she muttered.

"You don't know how good it was?" Joanne clarified. "Or, you don't know if you want to share?"

Oh, these women! They were like a pack of dogs with a bone. No wonder Jeremy took off. Resolutely, she admitted the truth. "I don't know how he kisses because I haven't kissed him."

"I thought y'all went walking in the moonlight," Marianne said, a faint frown marring her features. "Mayor Kincaid even saw you two holding hands."

"We were, but we didn't kiss."

All three women looked crestfallen and Dinah almost admitted she felt the same way.

"Hmph. I would have thought Jeremy would have more gumption than that," Joanne said with a frown.

"I wonder what's wrong with him," Mary Beth added. "Maybe he was sick?"

Just as Marianne was about to add her comment, Dinah spoke. "He wanted to . . . I didn't let him."

Again, three women stared at her in surprise. Surprised and more than a little disappointed. "Why not, Dinah? Do you really not like him?" Mary Beth asked.

"I do . . . but I'm trying not to." She turned to Joanne, looking for anyone to save her from the bottomless pit of a conversation. "You, of all people should know what I'm talking about. Don't you think Jeremy should be around someone younger?"

Joanne squirmed. "Me? Well, I admit that at first I was a little worried about the age difference . . . but now I don't think it matters. I know he's been attracted to you since he saw you at the grocery store."

"But five years' difference . . ."

"Years from now it won't matter at all," Marianne said. "Not after you two get married and start your own family."

"We're not getting married," Dinah protested, feeling like she was stuck in the center of a tornado. "I don't know if we're even going to go out on a date."

Again all three women were confused. "He really is a great guy," Mary Beth said, ready to defend him. "And he's different than most men his age. Jeremy's the kind of guy who plans for everything. He's steady. And a hard worker. If you're afraid he's going to be saying good-bye to you and go out with some co-ed, I just don't see it happening."

"I don't see it either," Joanne admitted, "and to tell the truth, at first I didn't think the two of you would be right for each other."

Dinah handed Bryan his sippy cup and another twenty Cheerios™ when he started to fuss in her lap. "So what's changed your mind?"

"Seeing how you look at each other. Like you're dying to stare at each other, but afraid of what the other might do."

"I haven't been staring at him."

"But you've been going out of your way not to," Joanne pointed out. "That's telling."

"Dear, I'm not saying Jeremy Reece is the one for

you, but I do certainly feel that he could be," Marianne said kindly. "Don't let what-ifs overtake you."

Dinah stared out at the street, recalled the faint sheen of color that stained his face and neck as he left. What had he been feeling? Probably not anything good. "I don't think he's going to ask me again. He said he was going to wait on me."

"Then ask him out."

She stared at the ladies in surprise. "You don't think that would be ridiculous, like some old woman coming on to him?"

"You're twenty-eight, not sixty-eight, so stop acting like you're approaching retirement," Joanne said. "And second, who cares if someone does think you're too old for him or he's too young for you? All that matters is when the two of you are alone."

Mary Beth chuckled at Joanne's words. "Dinah, go ask him out. You'll be glad you did."

She was almost convinced she should do that, and wasn't sure if she was proud of herself or ashamed. "Where?"

"Ask him over to dinner," Mary Beth suggested. "Missy did that with Kevin. Remember, Jo?"

Joanne's expression turned dreamy. "Oh yeah, the night after Kevin had dinner at Missy's we all were together, and it was all Kevin could talk about. You would have thought she was a personal chef and interior decorator by the way he gushed about her."

"What did she fix for him?"

Mary Beth grinned. "Chicken."

"Chicken?"

"He would have eaten sawdust and gushed," Joanne explained, holding her arms out to Bryan. "It was the company he cared about, Dinah," she said, glancing at the little boy. "Ask him over for dinner."

She sighed. She had been hurt when Jeremy walked out that door, and knew the only way she was going to feel happy was when she could look forward to see him. "I'm going to do it. I'm going to ask him over for dinner," she stated. "That is ... if y'all are sure you don't mind?"

"We want you to!" The three other women at the table practically yelled.

But she still felt awkward. Though she knew she was just as nervous about dating again as she was about Jeremy, it seemed as if every insecurity she'd ever had was now smothering her in waves. "And his parents? You don't think they'll think it's strange?"

"I'll take care of them," Marianne said. "You call him up tonight."

For some reason, calling, then asking Jeremy's father to get him on the phone felt scary.

"Or, you could stop by the club," Mary Beth said brightly.

"I can do that," Dinah said, then finally grinned as she gazed at the other women. "I'm going to ask him today."

"Well, hallelujah," Marianne McKinley said, speaking for all of them. "I'm glad that's taken care of."

Chapter Nine

"So you see, it's not just roast beef and lasagna we're talking about," Payton explained to Jeremy after he cornered him at the back table. "It's that Priscilla has a whole host of dreams and talents that she thinks is going to waste."

Jeremy set down the water pitcher as best he could, though a major part of him felt like dumping the whole thing in Payton's lap. The guy was totally, completely smitten with Priscilla, and couldn't seem to veer conversation along any other tangent.

All roads led to her. And Jeremy—who had some girl trouble of his own, thank you very much—was getting a little tired of hearing about it. "Let Priscilla out of the contract," he said, somewhat spitefully.

"Then you'd be free to date her and she could cook what she wanted."

Payton rolled his eyes. "Yeah, right."

"What's wrong with that idea?"

"Just about everything. Priscilla's not going to stay around here if she's free."

This guy was so screwed up, it was amazing he could survive on his own. "In case you haven't checked lately, I'll remind you that this isn't the 1800s. You don't own her."

Payton puffed up his heavily starched, white button-down-covered chest. "I practically do. She has a contract with me."

"With the club."

"With the club." Payton sighed and slouched down in his chair, a sure sign that he was depressed. "I just don't know what I'm going to tell her about the annual Father's Day buffet. The men in the club are going to expect roast beef and lasagna. They come for roast beef and lasagna."

"But Priscilla doesn't want to make it?"

"Not really. She actually suggested that we have a barbecue out by the pool instead, grill steaks, hot dogs, chicken, fish."

For the life of him, Jeremy couldn't see why this was causing a problem. "What's wrong with that? I'd go to that Father's Day buffet."

Payton stared hard at him. "That's because you're

not Baron McKinley or your dad. Those men thrive on tradition."

"Sometimes change is good."

"Sometimes a lot of things are good," Payton replied with a disgruntled look. "Doesn't mean you have to do them."

Talking to Payton was like talking to a wall. As deftly as he could, Jeremy excused himself to make the rounds around the area, offering water and tea to the ladies at table seven who just finished golfing.

Of course, that led to conversation about his parents, his sister's baby, and his new job. He was just finishing his rounds when Dinah wandered in, looking determined. Just the sight of her made his afternoon a little bit brighter.

He ambled over to her. "Hi. What brings you here?"

She gazed at him, her brown eyes wide and cautious, and for a minute he thought she was going to turn right back around. Especially when it became evident that the golfing ladies were more than eager to eavesdrop on every word.

"Let's go over here," he murmured, setting the pitcher of water down on an empty table and guiding Dinah toward the sliding glass doors that led to the patio. "I'm taking a five minute break," he called out to Payton, who nodded right back.

As soon as they were outside, he seated himself across from her at a wrought-iron table. "What's up?"

Dinah bit her lip. "I'm sorry. I don't know what I

was thinking, coming here while you were working." She paused for breath, then looked even more confused. "Why are you working, by the way? I thought you were going home."

"I left The Mill in such a hurry I forgot that I didn't have a car. Thought I'd put in a few hours and then get a ride home with Payton or Priscilla."

She nodded her understanding, though she did look completely preoccupied. "Oh."

He waited again, glanced through the glass door to make sure nothing out of the ordinary was happening. "Did you need something?"

She leaned forward, the ends of her hair falling toward her jaw. "Actually, no. I mean, I was *wanting* something. I mean I'd like . . ." Her voice drifted off, in sync with the color rising in her cheeks.

Immediately, worry set in. "Is something wrong with Bryan? Is that why he's not here?"

"Oh no. He's with Joanne and Mary Beth, actually." She flashed a smile. "I'm trying to ask you something, and I'm embarrassed to say it's a little hard in coming."

Wearily Jeremy waited. She was probably going to tell him to leave her alone. That she didn't need to have to worry about him making calves' eyes at her. He steeled himself to look completely at ease, like he got rejected all the time. "Just say it, then," he coaxed. "That's usually the best way."

"I guess so. Well, all right, then. Would you like to

come over next Saturday night for dinner?" she asked quickly.

He was completely taken aback. She was asking him out? To her house for dinner? It took all the control he had to not stand up and cheer. "Sure," he said as easily as possible. "That sounds really nice."

"Bryan will be there."

Where else would he be? "I hope so."

She smiled then, perking her face up and making him grin in return. "I thought we could grill steaks."

"Steaks sound great."

"And potatoes. Salad, too."

He couldn't resist any longer. Reaching out, he clasped one of the hands that gripped the edge of the table and enfolded it in his own. "Anything you do would make me happy."

Brown eyes darkened, looking almost black. He could stare at them forever. Because she looked in need of further coaxing, he added, "Really."

"You're not just saying that?"

"I'm not just saying that," he replied. "Thank you for inviting me."

Dinah let out a deep breath. "I was a little nervous. I was afraid you'd say no."

"I didn't," he said lightly, though he knew he'd would never deny her anything. For a brief moment he wondered if he was in love with her. Was that what love was like? Did it just sneak up on a person, making him want to do anything for a woman, just to see her smile?

He slid his fingers through her own, taking a minute to notice the difference between their two hands . . . his so much meatier, bigger, tanner. Rough. Her hand felt delicate and smooth in his own. And cold.

"Are you chilly?"

"No," she said, with a smile. "I'm just fine."

So was he. "I better go get back to work. What time on Saturday?"

She thought for a moment. "Is five too early? Bryan goes to bed at 7:30. If it's any later, you'd hardly get to see him."

"Five's just fine."

"Well, then. I guess I better get on back. Bryan needs a snack, and then I've got to go to the store. And sew a few costumes."

"I forgot you were doing them. How's it going?"

She shrugged. "It's going. I'll be ready for your first fitting in a few weeks."

"I'll be ready," he said as they slowly left the patio and entered the dining room.

As she walked away, he picked up his water pitcher again, feeling ready to conquer anything. Even ask Priscilla or Payton for a ride home.

Dinah knew inviting Jeremy over had been a mistake. A silly, thoughtless mistake. The only problem was that she didn't know how to get out of it at all. One more time she wrote down her grocery list only to immediately cross each item off. Although she'd never claim to be a gourmet, she could certainly handle grilling steaks and putting together a salad. She just didn't quite know what to do about dessert. It seemed the most personal item, and because it seemed that way to her, it embarrassed her too.

She didn't know his tastes. Cherry or apple pie? Maybe a chocolate cake? Cookies, ice cream?

Something fancy to make up for the plain dinner?

She sighed, wishing Betty Crocker would appear before her in a blaze of glory. But then the door opened, and the next best thing did: Priscilla Hayward, gourmet cook extraordinaire. Dinah couldn't believe her luck.

"Hi, Priscilla," she called out, while Bonnie barked out a cheerful greeting.

"Hi," Priscilla said, after petting Bonnie. "Have we met?"

"Only in passing."

Relief cascaded over her pretty features. "Thank goodness. I've met so many people, and I'm afraid to offend anyone by admitting that I don't remember their name."

"I'm Dinah Cate, and you've met my parents, the Ryans, I believe."

Recognition brightened her eyes as Priscilla placed her. "Now I've got it." She laughed. "I'm sorry, I still can't quite get used to knowing everyone everywhere I go."

"I understand," Dinah said. "Is there anything I can help you with?"

Priscilla named a few authors. "I love their books. Any new ones out?"

"Let's go see," Dinah replied. "I think Arnold Fergusen's new mystery is out in hardcover." For the next few minutes they wandered through the shelves, discussing books and authors. Priscilla was just the kind of customer Dinah liked: a chatty one.

Most people enjoyed being by themselves when selecting novels, and Dinah understood that, but there was nothing she liked more than conversing about authors and titles with someone new. Even if their tastes were completely opposite, she got a charge just from the interaction.

Finally Priscilla had an armful of books and a happy smile on her face. "I'm so glad Joanne told me about this place," she said as she walked to Dinah's front counter. "It's been a pleasure to be here."

"I'm glad you came."

After ringing up the order, she knew it was now or never. Priscilla was genuinely nice and was so pretty that she probably dated all the time. If anyone could help her plan the meal it would be her. "Do you have a minute? Would you like a cup of coffee?"

"Sure."

Eagerly, Dinah hopped up and fixed two steaming

mugs and brought them to the front of the store. "I need some help with a dinner I'm planning."

"Ah," Priscilla said, understanding dawning. "Big party or small?"

"Small. I invited someone over for dinner. We're having steaks, baked potatoes, and salad. Rolls."

"Sounds like a male guest."

Dinah laughed at the description. "You guessed it."

"Guys love that kind of food. What's the problem?"

"Dessert."

A smile played on Priscilla's lips. "Dessert?"

"I don't know what to fix. I don't know what he would like. Any ideas?"

Priscilla sipped her coffee as she studied Dinah over the rim. "A couple. Fancy or simple?"

"Simple."

"How about ice cream sundaes?"

"Really?"

Priscilla laughed. "Why do you look so shocked?"

"Well, you've got this amazing reputation, I was expecting you to say crepes Suzette or Baked Alaska, or something."

"I could suggest those, if you wanted to cook all day, but I think simple desserts are sometimes best. Crush up some Oreos, pecans, a candy bar. Have out a topping or two. Your guest is going to love it!"

"That's all you would do?"

"Sure."

"Really?"

"Well, if I was showing off, I'd make the ice cream and the sauce, and put it all in some kind of fancy bowls. But it's the same thing. Anyway, I have a feeling that your guest isn't coming over for dinner to critique you," she said, smiling at Dinah.

"I don't think he is," Dinah confided.

"And why would he? You're adorable."

Dinah laughed. "Thanks." Then, because talking about it with someone who wasn't related to herself or Jeremy felt so good, she said, "Speaking of my guest . . . Well, he's younger than me."

Priscilla raised her jet black eyebrows a fraction. "Now that's interesting."

That didn't sound good. "Do you think that's bad?"

"Not at all. I think if you have found someone who you like being with, and he feels the same way, you should hold onto him tight."

Dinah laughed. "Ever felt that way?"

She raised a shoulder. "Once or twice."

"And . . . now?" she prodded, recalling the fireworks that Jeremy had said had been going on between Payton and Priscilla.

Priscilla looked taken aback. "Now? Gosh, who knows. I'm enormously attracted to a guy who dresses better than most women, who can lie at the drop of a hat, and who has the whitest teeth of anyone I've ever met."

"That's quite a lot to deal with."

"Tell me about it! And . . . he follows me around and gives me compliments."

Dinah wrinkled her nose and tried to sound appalled. "I'd hate that."

Priscilla chuckled. "I know. He sounds perfect, doesn't he? If only he hadn't lied to me about Payton. Then I might give him a chance."

Intrigued, Dinah leaned forward. "Well, what did he say?"

"He led me to believe Payton, Ohio was completely different than it is. That it was progressive, and upbeat." She rolled her eyes. "Those things it is not."

Dinah felt vaguely sad to hear her hometown derided. "It really is a good place to live."

Priscilla looked stricken. "Oh, don't get me wrong, I'm loving it here. It's just . . . well, I was hoping to make a name for myself. To go back to Houston, Texas a hot-shot chef, and use my reputation to start my own bistro." She shook her head. "No offense, but it's not going to happen here."

Dinah wasn't offended. "What are you going to do?"

"At first I was just going to quit. But now . . . I don't know. I'm liking the club a lot. And the board members, with all their motherly and fatherly advice, have kind of grown on me. And then there's Payton Chase."

"You know, I've always liked him. He was really

sweet to me when my husband died. I don't know what I would have done without friends like him."

Priscilla stared at her in surprise. "I'm sorry about your husband."

So was she. "It's okay. It was a few years ago."

"So this dating stuff is pretty new, huh?" Priscilla asked, her voice kindhearted.

"Yeah. Yes, it is."

"Would you like me to make something spectacular for you?"

"Thanks, but no. I'm actually looking forward to the sundaes. And I think Jeremy will like them too."

Priscilla's smile became full-fledged. "Jeremy Reece?"

"Yes."

"Oh, Dinah," Priscilla said with a sigh. "He's practically dreamy. You're going to have a wonderful time."

Chapter Ten

Dinner was going to be a disaster. Bryan was crying, the salad from the bag looked wilted, and even after an hour, the potatoes still weren't soft. Dinah frantically wondered if Jeremy would mind if she just handed him the keys to her sedan and told him to take her away.

Somehow she thought he just might run away if she did that!

"It's okay, Bry," she cooed, holding him on her hip like she used to when he was about five pounds lighter. "Everything's going to be okay."

But he only squirmed and wiggled, wanting instead to play in front of the oven. Even Bonnie had gotten into the act, howling every time Bryan let out an especially loud cry.

Dinah felt like crying herself. Here she'd been so ready to have a perfect dinner, to show Jeremy just how fun being around her and Bryan could be, when all the elements in the world seemed determined to fight her left and right.

With despair, she glanced down at her white capris and bright yellow top. Both were now splattered with who-knew-what, and looked wrinkled enough to have been slept in. Yeah, he was going to be impressed, all right.

The doorbell rang, and with a grimace she realized that not only was Jeremy on time, but he also had that annoying male trait of not realizing that you never, ever arrived at a party early. Holding Bryan tightly on her hip, she went to greet him, as well as she was able.

"Hey," he said. "I hope you don't mind that I'm a few minutes early. I didn't want to be late, and then the traffic through downtown was nonexistent, and I didn't want your neighbors to think I was casing the neighborhood . . ." His voice drifted off as he caught sight of her stricken face and Bryan's tear-streaked one. "What's wrong?"

"Everything," she wailed. "Nothing's gone right. Everything's gone wrong, and I wanted it to be so nice for you," she said, leading him to the back of the kitchen. "I can't seem to do anything easily and Bryan must notice that I'm not myself, because he keeps fussing and crying." She stomped her foot when Bry grabbed a handful of her hair and pulled. "No, Bry," she murmured, then turned to Jeremy. "I guess you want to leave, huh?"

Jeremy looked at her, stunned. She might have thought everything was wrong, but he'd heard enough to know that things were just fine. If she wanted things to be nice for him, then she cared. And that was enough.

And she looked adorable in those snug capris, even if they were stained with what looked to be Spaghetti Os. "I don't want to leave," he said slowly, then held out his arms to Bryan since it looked as if Dinah was about to tilt to one side from the boy's weight.

"Come here, sport."

With a solemn face, Bryan reached for him, and held on tight, quieting at once.

Bonnie trotted over and positioned her head right under his hand. He followed the beagle's wishes, gave her a few pats, then watched the dog pad over to her canvas covered bed and lie down.

Pleased to be helping so much, he glanced at Dinah, ready to hear her approval.

Dinah looked at him like he was a traitor. "How did you do that?" she asked.

"I like dogs," he said, motioning to Bonnie. "And as for Bryan, well . . . I've got a niece. He must know I'm anxious to see another guy." He cooed to Bryan again, then turned to Dinah. "How can I help?"

She chuckled. "You already have." Briefly she told

him the menu, and described the variety of troubles she'd had even preparing the simple meal. "Would you mind being in charge of the steaks? You could grill them outside, and Bryan would probably play just fine in his sandbox if you were out there."

"Show me the way," he said. After a few minutes, the steaks were on, Bryan was occupied putting sand into a bucket, and Dinah walked out to sit with him, two glasses of tea in her hands.

"This is more how I was hoping things would be."

He tilted his head, watching her, ready to listen to everything she said. "How?"

"I was hoping we could relax, enjoy the evening."

He already was enjoying himself, but because she seemed so worried, he tried to set her at ease once again. "I am enjoying myself, Dinah. Believe me, I grew up with four siblings. Dinner time can be the trickiest time of the day."

She laughed. "I guess so. It was in our house, too. My mom is a terrible cook, and my dad was always trying to find ways not to eat her concoctions."

Jeremy burst out laughing. "You almost sound proud of him!"

"I was! My brother Ben and I would stare at the goulash or casserole that she'd dished on our plates and try to think of new ways to give it to the dog."

"Did it work?"

"Sometimes. Skip, our beagle back then, was real found of liver meatballs."

"Eww!"

Dinah made a face. "Eww is right. I'm not much of a cook, but all the things I can make are easily recognizable."

"Well, I'm a great cook, so you won't have to worry," he teased, then froze as she stared at him hard. He needed to watch his words better or he was going to scare her off before he had a chance to get close to her. "I mean, if I ever cook you dinner."

"I'll keep that in mind."

"So . . . any other dark secrets?" he asked next, eager to know more about her.

"Hmm," she said, "not really. I'm a reasonable housekeeper, an excellent book store owner, and have been known to spend too much on cute outfits for Bryan." She sipped her tea then leaned forward. "What about you?"

He shrugged. "I like old cars, old houses, good steaks, and . . . pretty blonds." He smiled when color rose to her cheeks, but he didn't even consider taking his words back. There was something about her that told him that she had heard compliments too little in recent times. And he wasn't going to let her pretend that he was over merely because he needed another friend. He had friends, and lots of them. At that moment he wanted to be around Dinah, wanted to finally kiss her.

"I like blonds, too," she said, ducking her head away before he could scrutinize her face.

He didn't know what to say to that. Something told him that it wasn't the time to flirt anymore. Only two topics seemed safe: Bryan or the steaks.

Luckily Bryan was on the same wavelength. He toddled over, one fist full of sand. With a fierce shake, it fell to the ground and on his feet. "Ack!" he said triumphantly.

"No, Bry, that was not great," Dinah reproved.

Because the little boy was standing in front of him, just waiting to be acknowledged, Jeremy scooped him up in his arms. "Hey, big guy. What's up?"

That seemed to be all the opening he needed. Bryan squirmed out of his arms, then held out a chubby hand, obviously wanting Bryan to follow him to the sandbox. All the while he chattered in baby-talk, about one out of every third word intelligible.

"He wants you to see his trucks," Dinah translated. "Be careful, though. Bryan's a true believer of examining things while standing in the sandbox."

"I can do that," Jeremy said, already slipping off his loafers and socks and rolling up the hem of his jeans two times. "Let's go, Bryan."

Bryan smiled widely, then hopped back in, motioning for Jeremy to sit right next to him.

Dinah watched Jeremy and Bryan with something approaching awe. It was so rare for her son to actively choose to be around men, and really rare for it to happen so quickly.

And, she imagined, it also wasn't a very common

occurrence for men to discard their shoes and socks with such happy abandon and plop down in the middle of a sandbox. But that's what Jeremy was doing, and he looked to be having a great time loading up dump trucks.

Becoming aware that she was staring, Dinah cleared her throat. "I'm just going to put the rest of the meal on the table."

"Okay," Jeremy said, barely looking up.

Feeling strangely left out, Dinah flipped the steaks, then prepared the rest of the food. Fifteen minutes later everyone was washing their hands.

And a half hour after that, Dinah couldn't believe that dinner was over; Bryan looked about ready to fall asleep at the table, and she had a whole mess to still clean up. All that effort for thirty minutes of dining!

"I liked the sundaes," Jeremy said, pushing his bowl away. "It's been awhile since I had one."

"Thanks. I thought they were good, too," she commented, though she couldn't help but think that the ice cream all over Bryan wasn't going to come off easily.

"I'll work on the dishes, Di," Jeremy said, startling her out of her daze. "You go clean Bryan up and put him to bed."

"You don't mind?"

"Not in the slightest." He chuckled and gestured toward her countertops. "Besides, I think there's going to be plenty left for you, too."

She had to agree. She'd taken just about every dish out of her cupboards to make, bake, and serve everything. Somewhat grumpily she realized that her mother, and probably Jeremy, could have made do with about a third of the equipment.

With a sigh, she picked up Bryan, quickly washed his face with a washcloth, put him in his pajamas, and tucked him in bed. He was asleep before she left the room.

"Back already?"

"I am. I think you wore him out!"

"Glad I could help," he said, handing her a bowl to dry. "We'll get this done in no time."

Silently they washed and dried the mountain of dishes, stacking some in the dishwasher, hand washing and drying others. Bonnie wandered around the kitchen, poking her nose under the countertops, looking for scraps.

As they neared the end, a sense of calmness floated through her. "This was nice," she said. "I'm so glad you came over."

He leaned back against the counter. "What do you usually do now, after dinner, when Bryan is asleep?"

She was surprised by the question. "Not too much. Watch TV. Relax. Read a little bit. Laundry."

He tilted his head. "Where do you sit?"

"In there."

He took her hand. "Come on, then."

Within minutes, Dinah found herself sitting on the couch next to Jeremy, shoes off, legs tucked under her. And right then and there . . . she was back in time.

No bills or babies to worry about. No stack of mail or baby clothes to fold.

Nope. Right then, right there, all she could seem to think about was whether her hair looked okay, if the guy beside her thought she was cute . . . if he was ever going to kiss her good night.

As if in response, Jeremy dropped an arm across her back, his warm hand cupping her shoulder in a way that brought back memories of drive-ins and football games.

He chuckled. "I'm sorry. For some reason I keep wanting to look over my shoulder to see if your dad is going to catch us on the couch."

"I've been thinking that this feels kind of funny, too."

His hand raised. "Do you want me to move?"

"No," she said, then cursed her tongue. Was it really necessary to sound that desperate?

But if Jeremy thought she sounded funny, he gave no indication. In fact, he scooted a little closer. Played with the curls at the end of her hair. "Have I thanked you for inviting me over yet?"

"Have I thanked you for not leaving when you saw what a state I was in?"

He smiled. "I'm kind of glad I found you like that.

Made me feel like you weren't quite as perfect as I thought you were."

It was all she could do not to stare at him in surprise. "You thought I was perfect?"

"Uh huh." His fingers brushed her bare skin, giving her goose bumps and a faint tremor in her stomach. "Maybe if I asked again, you might consider going out with me?"

It was hard to think clearly when his body was so close to her own; when he smelled so good, like expensive cologne from the department store, when his fingers brushed the delicate skin around her collar bone, sending shockwaves straight to her heart.

She knew she was going to die if he didn't kiss her within two seconds.

She glanced at his eyes. Silvery blue, vividly awaiting her, with the patience of a saint . . . or at least a really good person. "I would," she said softly.

With a sigh, she felt his shoulders relax. And then, he was curving toward her, leaning in, cupping her jaw in his hands.

And kissing her so tenderly, like she was perfect for him.

Every sensation in her body shifted to high gear. His lips were soft yet firm; his hands, so gentle as his thumbs caressed her cheeks, then wrapped around her back.

He smelled like cologne, but like Jeremy, too. Full

of soap and man ... and all with the slight hint of Bryan. And he tasted even better.

She never, ever wanted such a kiss to end. He felt too good. And she felt too fresh. Too aware of him. Too new.

And then finally he pulled away, but only inches, only enough to meet her gaze head on. And smiled.

Chapter Eleven

"What are you doing, son?"

Jeremy looked up from the small mountain of folders and batches of paperwork that he'd been trying to get a handle on. "Trying to figure out where I've hidden another ten thousand dollars," he said with a sigh.

"Any luck?"

"Nope." He dragged a hand through his hair and wondered how much he dared to share with his dad. He wanted advice, not for things to be fixed. Sometimes his dad didn't seem to see the difference. Since the desire for his dad's experience and wisdom outweighed anything else, he decided to give it a try. "I found a house. Did you hear about that?"

"A little," his dad said, sitting down across from

him at their kitchen table. "But I was hoping to hear about it from you."

"It's great," Jeremy said, completely aware that he sounded suspiciously like he had back in tenth grade when he'd found an electric guitar on sale and was sure he needed it in order to be a star. "It's run-down, and sprawling, and made of stone. Big oak trees practically fill up the back yard. Beautiful woodwork in the den."

"Sounds good."

Jeremy nodded. "It is . . ." His voice drifted off, uncertain of how to tell his father that he couldn't afford it.

"But . . . ?"

"But, it's a little more than I would like. And I'm worried if I wait too long, it's going to be gone, but if I give in and get it, I'm not going to have a thing left in my savings account."

His dad glanced at a few of the papers, too. "I can see your problem. Guess you've already talked to Payton about working more hours?" he asked, leaning back.

"Yeah. He said he could maybe fit in five hours more a week on the schedule. That's not going to make a whole lot of difference."

His dad smirked. "Especially if Payton and Priscilla are still at it."

Jeremy laughed. "You should see them together. They are slowly driving me mad. Priscilla could say the sky is blue and still Payton would find a way to argue about it." He sighed. "Any ideas?"

"A few. You're the only child we've had who managed to hold a part time job during all of college, save like crazy, and graduate early." He grinned, his eyes twinkling.

Jeremy stared at him, surprised. He'd never accomplished those things in order to receive praise, he'd just done them because he couldn't imagine functioning any other way. He believed in hard work and savings, and always had. "I have some money saved, and there is money I made substitute teaching last spring. And the tutoring." He shook his head in frustration. "I don't think there's enough to go buy a house and furnish it, though."

"Interest rates are awfully low."

"Not that low, Dad."

He gazed at Jeremy again. "Somewhere in the midst of your hard work, I bet we saved some money. How about a loan?"

Jeremy winced. This was what he'd been afraid of. "No thanks."

"Because?"

"Because I want to look at this place and know it is mine."

His dad looked incredulous. "It will be. Believe me, your mom and I don't want to live there with you."

Jeremy burst out laughing. "I don't want you to! No, it's just that there's something else . . ."

"Ah."

Jeremy organized the papers again until they were in a neat pile then spoke. "This girl I met . . . Dinah. I like her a lot, Dad."

"I know Dinah. Know her parents, too."

"She had me over for dinner the other night." Jeremy smiled at the memory. "Everything was a mess, but together we made it okay. I helped with Bryan, then she put him to bed and we did the dishes. I . . . I had a great time." He paused, well aware that he had put himself out for ridicule. Hadn't he heard more than once that he should be having a good time? Dating lots of cute girls? Living more carefree?

This was just the opportunity his parents loved to take advantage of. Before he knew it, they would be reminding him of his age, how he should be doing the things that Kevin and Cameron did when they were fresh out of college.

As if the Reece kids needed to be carbon-copies of each other.

But his dad only folded his hands on the table and looked wistful. "Your mom and I have had some great times just being home. I've done my share of dishes with her, discussing the day's events." He smiled at the memories. "Sometimes it's nice to do that. So . . . you're serious about her?"

Jeremy swallowed, thanking the fates for finally giving him a person who really wanted to know how he was feeling . . . not just tell him what they thought. "Yeah. I'm serious about her, Dad." There. It was out in the open.

"And the baby . . . ?"

"He's amazing."

"You don't mind the responsibility?"

He shook his head.

"I should have known. You never have, son."

"What do you think I should do about the house?"

His dad shrugged. "Don't know. I've lots of ideas, but something tells me that you'll figure it out in your own time." He leaned back and shared a smile with Jeremy as they heard his mom open the back door, followed by a rustling of what could only be shopping bags. "Ah, looks like your mom's back."

Jeremy grinned. His mom was always carting in bags from somewhere. "In two minutes, she'll hear our voices and come in, telling us where she's been."

"Two minutes after, she'll suggest we either grill some steaks or go out to eat."

"Because it's just too nice to stay inside," Jeremy finished. "And she's so worn out from fighting the crowds."

They shared a smile. "Bring over Dinah and Bryan one day soon. We'd like to get to know her."

Jeremy glanced at the stack of paperwork again. "And you really don't have any idea about the house? I'm afraid I'm going to lose it if I wait too long."

His dad shrugged. "I guess the pros and cons of living there would depend on who you want to live there with, wouldn't you say?"

"I never thought of that."

"You might want to," his dad said just as his mom's clipping heels headed in their direction. "Some day, someone might want to be there with you . . . and then you'll find a way to make it happen, even if it means asking me for help." He stood up then, just as his mom charged in, a shopping bag in each hand. "Darling, you're home."

"Jim, Jeremy, you wouldn't believe where I've been," Daphne gushed. "Kenwood Mall!"

Jim winked at Jeremy. "What did you find?"

"Oh, I'll show you everything, but I just realized it's almost dinner! Jeremy, are you working?"

"No."

"Well, let's either grill or go out. It's just too nice to stay inside."

"We were just thinking that, honey. We'll do whatever you want."

Without pretense, his mom kissed his dad right then and there on the mouth. "Oh, honey."

Jeremy could almost imagine Dinah and himself in their places.

The uniform was thick wool, and dark navy in color. Two rows of brass buttons lined the jacket, and frayed bits of braid and embroidery decorated the shoulders. It looked to fit a man who was smaller than today's regular-sized man, but maybe that was simply her own thoughts, making the Civil War soldiers seem far larger than life.

But no matter what the reason, Dinah was glad she was visiting the historical museum, and seeing the special uniforms of the Union infantry. Though she'd been following the pattern Joanne had given her, just seeing the actual clothing soldiers wore gave her new insight into how they would need to look.

The last three weeks had been busy. She'd divided her time between working at the store, caring for Bryan, and sewing the costumes.

And thinking about Jeremy.

He'd stopped by the store every few days, and once they'd even gone to The Grill for burgers. Things between them were good . . . and more than a little disconcerting. She felt so many things for Jeremy: desire, friendship, wariness. It was going to be a relief when she could finally sort through her mixed-up emotions.

Scribbling notes on paper, she hardly heard Joanne and Missy join her. "Aren't these incredible?" Joanne gushed. "I'm so thankful for Mr. Henry for letting us put them on display this month."

"They are incredible," Dinah admitted, smiling at Missy. "Like I said, I've been getting those costumes done. Even though they aren't quite the work of art that these are, I think you'll be pleased. Jeremy's going to come over this afternoon before work and try his on."

"I bet he's going to look great in it. You know, the other uniform is for Kevin."

"I thought you said your husband was going to be too busy."

"He thinks he is, but he might attend for Joanne."

Dinah chuckled. "He might attend for you, Missy. I have a feeling he'd do just about anything for you . . . but then, we both know that."

"Even if he would go, I'm not sure if I'm going to ask him. Dressing up is just not his thing."

Dinah glanced at the clock above the door. Four o'clock. "Are you about to close?"

"We are. We close early on Thursdays to have a board meeting."

"I'll get out of your way, then."

"You're not in our way," Joanne said quickly. "Besides, I don't want you to do a thing until you tell us how dinner went."

Dinah suddenly recalled how Joanne had spoken of Missy's dinner for her husband with reverent tones. "Not quite as nice as I heard yours was, Missy. The house was a mess, Bryan was crying, and I was a nervous wreck."

"You?"

"Me."

"What did Jeremy do?"

"Everything. Grilled steaks, played with Bryan. Helped with the dishes." She grimaced at the memory. Poor Jeremy had probably been thinking he couldn't get out of her life fast enough.

Missy sighed. "He's a great guy. Just like his brother."

Dinah wasn't about to disagree. She had enjoyed being with him, and the part of the evening they'd spent on the couch had been awfully nice. Feeling daring, she said, "And you can tell Mary Beth that she was right. He is a dreamboat."

Joanne clapped her hands together. "I'm so pysched you told me before her. Mary Beth had been teasing Dinah, wanting to know how Jeremy kissed," she said to Missy.

Missy perked her head up. "Well?"

"I kiss very well, thank you," Jeremy said from the doorway.

Dinah's drawing pad fell to the ground. "Oh my gosh. I didn't hear you."

"I hope not. I'd hate to think you wanted me to hear you talking about . . . me kissing?"

Joanne blushed as well. "Just girl talk, little brother," she said quickly. "Now go take this girl of yours out of here so I can get some work done."

Dinah wished Joanne would just toss her over the stair railing, she was so embarrassed. "What are you doing here? I thought we were going to meet in an hour."

He let her lead the way down the stairs, then answered her as they walked outside to the parking lot. "I called your mom and she said you were here. I'm going to have to postpone our fitting. Work."

"I thought you waited tables all night last night?"

"I did. Plus I asked Payton for a few more hours."

The day was so beautiful, she didn't see any reason to postpone their conversation. "Why?"

He hung his head. "I'm really loving that house I told you about. And . . . I don't quite have enough in savings to cover the down payment and everything else I want to do."

Understanding dawned. "Oh. Gosh, that's such a shame, though. I mean, about the fitting."

"Maybe we could do the fitting late tonight? Or tomorrow morning?"

She thought quickly. "How about in the morning? That way I'll be wide awake and Bryan won't be fussy."

Jeremy smiled in relief. "Great. Around eight?"

"Around eight."

"I'm glad you're not mad."

"I'm disappointed, not mad. I was kind of looking forward to seeing you."

"Really? That makes me happy." And with that, he took her hand. "You don't know how many times I've thought about kissing you again."

She had a pretty good idea. It was at least as much as the idea had popped into her head.

"I hope I'm not rushing you."

"No."

"And Sunday night? Will you and Bryan still come over for dinner?"

"We will."

"My parents can get a little . . . involved, but you'll like being around them."

"I'm sure I will."

"And I have a feeling at least one of my siblings will finagle a dinner invitation, too. And since all of them are married, that will be at least two more people." He looked at her steadily. "When my family gets together, things can get a little crazy."

"I'll consider myself warned." She said it in a way to make him smile, but it looked as thought Jeremy was about to do anything but.

"So you're sure about this? I don't want to do anything you don't want to."

"You won't."

Gray eyes glowed. "You're right. I . . . I really like you, Dinah." His cheeks colored. "What is it about you that makes me sound like such an idiot? I didn't mean to say it like that. I meant—"

But she didn't give him a minute to say anything. Quickly, she kissed him. Not hard, not especially passionate . . . but just enough for him to realize that she was right there with him, by choice.

And at that moment, there was nowhere she would rather be.

Chapter Twelve

"**Y**ou've sure been putting in a lot of hours, lately," Priscilla said to Jeremy just as he was taking a break.

"Yeah. Might as well bring a sleeping bag here."

She pointed to the circles under his eyes. "You do look pretty tired."

"I worked that wedding reception last night. The bride and groom were in no hurry to start their wedding night."

"They catered in, so I had the night off."

"Must have been nice for you." He glanced at Priscilla, noticed the concern in her eyes, so he decided to admit the whole truth about what had been going on with him. "I haven't been sleeping too well."

Priscilla blew the wisps of bangs from her eyes. "I haven't either! Isn't that something?"

"What's your excuse?"

Priscilla looked embarrassed. "Just trying to get used to the changes here, I guess."

"Things a lot different from Houston?"

"Like night and day. The job, anyway. The people are just as nice." She sipped on a soda. "Your turn."

"I'm trying to figure out my future."

She frowned. "I thought yours was already planned out. Won't you be teaching in the fall?"

"Yeah. It's not the job, it's all the other stuff."

"Such as . . ."

"Such as there's a house I found to live in that I really like, but I don't know if I can afford it."

"My experience has always been to be prudent, though I didn't do that with this job." She paused. "And what else?"

He swallowed. "Dinah."

"Ah. So we're really telling the truth now? Well, in that case, my thoughts have been turned to a certain blue-eyed man."

"Is he who you'd thought you'd fall in love with?"

Priscilla looked shocked. "Um . . . I don't think we're in love . . . and as for your question, no. No, he's not. What about you?"

"I've always been attracted to happy people. And she's as pretty as any girl I've ever met. But I feel like such an idiot when I'm around her, like I'm pretending to be someone I'm not."

"Who are you pretending to be?"

He felt his skin flush. "I don't know. I've always been confident, and she makes me feel insecure, inadequate . . . then that makes me feel worse."

"I don't know Dinah well, but I must say I'm surprised she makes you feel that way."

"Sometimes I think she feels that way, too."

"Who feels what way?" Payton asked as he poured himself a cup of coffee and joined them.

Priscilla blushed. "No one."

"Must have been someone," he prodded.

Fire entered her eyes just as her shoulders pulled back. "No one you know."

"I know more people than you," he pointed out.

"That's not necessarily true. You just know more people here."

Payton narrowed his eyes. "That's what we were talking about."

"No," she corrected. "You made a blanket statement. An incorrect one."

Jeremy glanced from one to the other. Like a ball in the tennis match, they seemed perfectly content to lob one-liners at the other with no signs of fatigue. "I better get back to work. Bye, guys!"

And before they could say another word, he took off.

* * *

"Hold still, Jeremy. I need to mark the places where I need to fix the seams."

"This itches."

"It's going to itch something fierce when you wear it for the reenactment."

He frowned. "Don't remind me. It's going to be as hot as can be. I'm going to have to give up a whole day's work at the club, too."

"I'll be there."

"You'll be the only reason the day won't be a complete washout."

The word made her think of possible good news. "Maybe it will rain?"

Jeremy managed to look even more miserable. "Haven't you heard? The real Civil War soldiers actually fought in the rain. Joanne says we'll do this reenactment rain or shine."

Dinah couldn't help but imagine how uncomfortable the real soldiers must have been, especially when hunger, weariness, and despair had set in. "We'll just have to hope for cool, sunny skies, and a quick battle."

"You're such an optimist. I sound like a spoiled kid next to you. Sorry."

As she smoothed the fabric across his broad shoulders and placed a pin in one or two of the seams, she shook her head. "You don't sound like that at all. Just like a guy who would rather be wearing shorts in ninety degree weather instead of a navy blue uniform."

Slowly he lowered his head to meet her gaze, and within moments Dinah felt transfixed, all over again. What was it about Jeremy that made her feel so young again? So carefree?

Probably his easy smile, beautiful eyes, and his lithe build.

And his kindness. His gentle way with Bryan. The sexy way he kissed, like he was savoring her.

She sighed. Whenever she thought of Jeremy, she couldn't help but feel a jolt to her heart, the kind she used to feel in seventh grade when Brad Franklin sat down beside her in homeroom. From that instant, nothing had existed but him. She'd forgotten the name of her teacher, her two friends she'd known from choir the year before. Brad had filled her world completely, even though all he'd done was smile.

That was how she felt around Jeremy, and the overwhelming puppy-love feelings made her feel scared and uncomfortable, like she was too old for such things but her body didn't realize that.

He shifted and looked away, then cleared his throat, making her sure that he was just as spellbound as she was. "Who's the other uniform for, again?"

"Well, it was for your brother Kevin, but now it's for Stratton Sawyer."

He grinned at that. "I knew Kevin was going to get out of it."

"Actually, Stratton seemed pretty excited about the idea."

Jeremy figured Stratton was just trying to please Joanne. "So . . . fitted him yet?"

"Only the basics. I took his measurements the other day. He's going to stop by the store one night next week to do this with me." She smoothed her hands down the length of his left leg, tried not to think about how muscular that leg felt, and began marking off the hem.

Jeremy's eyes turned stormy just as his left leg stiffened. "It doesn't bother you, doing all this . . . pinning?"

"Relax your leg. And not in the slightest," she said, bravely trying to ignore how her body was reacting to being so close to him. "I like to sew." She finished the marks, then stood up, circling Jeremy one more time.

"Maybe Joanne could help you with Stratton." His eyes lit up as she faced him again. "Or she could come with him!"

"Now why would she want to do that?" Dinah asked, smoothing the fabric along the planes of his back, then kneeling in front of him to check the line of the jacket.

His cheeks flushed. "I don't know."

Dinah bit her lip. What was bothering him? The idea of fitting Stratton's costume . . . or this particular fitting itself? Unable to help herself, she ran her fingers along his leg, from his knee on down. "Does this feel all right? I made it a little longer than normal, but I figured with your boots and all—"

Jeremy jerked his leg away. "Yes," he bit out. "Dinah, aren't we done yet?"

"I'm going as quickly as I can. What's wrong?"

"I don't know. I feel funny standing here with you kneeling at my feet," he said, and Dinah was amazed to see a faint line of red creep up his neck.

She couldn't resist teasing him. "And here I thought that was every man's dreams."

"Not mine. Dinah—"

She stood up. "I'm done," she said, unable to keep a few chuckles from escaping. "All you have to do now is get out of those clothes without removing any pins."

"Or sticking myself."

"Of course."

He padded away, grumbling, just as Bryan wandered over, his hands full of two plastic containers and a stuffed brown dog. "Jy?"

Dinah knelt down as he approached. "Jy's changing, but he'll be right back." She patted a spot next to her. "Show me what you got."

Bryan had just let her give his dog a hug when Jeremy appeared again. She watched him scan the room quickly for her, then his eyes light up when he spotted the two of them. Seeing such a reaction made her so happy. It was nice to know he didn't resent

Bryan's appearance. "We're over here," she called out. "Bry's been showing me his dog."

"Jy!" the little boy cried, dropping the dog and toddling over to Jeremy.

"Hey," he said, kneeling down on the floor as well. "You know my name."

Dinah laughed. He seemed to know just what to say. "I'm glad you came over this morning, even though we'll see each other tonight."

"Promise?"

"Promise. And not just because I wanted to get your costume done, either."

"That wasn't the only reason I stopped by, if you want to know the truth."

"I was thinking," she began, only to be interrupted by the doorbell ringing.

"I'll get it for you," Jeremy offered.

"Thanks."

Within minutes, he was leading Valerie into the family room, chatting with her about school and education courses. Bonnie followed them both, her tail wagging with pleasure.

"Hi, Dinah," Valerie said. "I forgot whether you wanted me this afternoon or not. Are you going to the store?"

Dinah almost couldn't think of a thing to say, she was so mesmerized by the sight of Jeremy and Valerie together. They looked so . . . right. Both about the same age. Both had bright-eyed, all-American good looks. Like a slap in the face, she was brought to the truth that once again, she had no business being with Jeremy Reece.

Realizing Valerie was waiting for a reply, she said quickly, "Oh, thanks, but it's okay. If I do go in, I'll take Bryan. The weather's not supposed to be that great, it will probably be really slow."

Valerie looked at her strangely. Then glanced at Jeremy as if she couldn't keep her eyes off of him. "Are you sure?"

"Positive." She cleared her throat, trying to sound peppy. "Um, gosh, Jeremy, did you go to Ohio State, too?"

"I did."

"I guess the two of you must have so much to catch up on, especially since Val is an education major."

He looked completely puzzled. "We'll have to talk all about that one day," he said to her politely.

Dinah grasped for another topic. "Oh, and I bet you two might have even gone to the same parties and didn't even realize it. Were you both in the Greek system?"

For the first time since she'd known Valerie, the girl treated her to a teen-aged look of disdain. "I was a Delta Gamma."

"Phi Delt," Jeremy said obediently.

A long, uncomfortable silence hung in the air. Dinah searched to think of anything else the two might have in common.

"I need to go," Valerie said, standing up abruptly. "See you tomorrow, Dinah?"

"Yes. At nine A.M., if you don't mind."

"I don't mind at all," Valerie said, bending down to give Bryan a hug. Bryan wrapped his chubby hands around her neck, gave her a wet kiss, then plopped back down to his set of bowls and containers.

With a sigh, Dinah watched her go.

Jeremy stood up. "I think I'll get going, as well."

"Are you sure? Would you like some coffee, or something?"

He shook his head no. "See you at six tomorrow?"

She scanned his face quickly. It was if someone had put a curtain over his eyes, they looked masked and distant. "Is something bothering you?"

If anything, his posture became more rigid. "Yeah, but it's nothing you need to worry about."

"I'm a good listener."

"Are you? I don't think you've heard one word I've said to you yet."

She stiffened at his sarcastic tone. "I don't think I understand."

After glancing at Bryan for a second, Jeremy stepped forward, lowered his voice. "Dinah, at the risk of sounding completely idiotic, I think I need to make myself as clear as possible. I like you."

Taken aback, she said, "I like you, too."

"No, not as a friend," he corrected, his gray-blue eyes stormy. "Not as Bryan's mom. I like you in every single kind of romantic way you can imagine. A lot. A whole lot. I know we haven't spent hours together. I know we need time to see if we can even have a relationship that can last, but I thought after our dinner the other night, after the times we've spent together over the last few weeks . . . that you felt the same way."

She closed her eyes. "I do."

"Do you? Then why in the world would you be pushing Valerie and me together?"

"I didn't do that," she protested, though her heart was telling her she certainly had.

"It felt that way to me. And to Valerie, I think. She kept looking at you like you were crazy."

"I just thought that maybe the two of you might want to get to know each other."

He exhaled slowly. "Why?"

His question caught her off-guard. "What do you mean, *why?*"

"Why do we want to get to know each other? Because I'm going to need to know Bryan's baby-sitter in the future? Because I need just one more college-aged girl as a friend?"

She looked away. "I don't know what I was thinking. She's just so cute, and sometimes I look at you and feel so old." She whispered the last part, embarrassed by both her behavior and her feelings. "I'm having a tough time admitting not only to myself but to other people how I feel about you."

Triumph gleamed in his eyes. "So . . . tell *me*. Say it out loud. How do you feel?"

She shrugged. "Smitten," she said, though she felt ridiculous even saying such a thing out loud. Lord, he must be thinking she was so silly.

He burst out laughing. "I'll take that."

She really wasn't following him. "What?"

He closed the space between the two of them and gripped her hand in his. "I'll take smitten. I'm smitten, too." Briefly he raised her hand and brushed his lips against her knuckles, the gallant gesture making her knees go weak. "See you tomorrow night?"

"I'll be there."

"I'm warning you, it will be crazy."

"I like crazy."

He laughed again, his voice ringing carefree and boyish. So charming. "Bye, Dinah. Bye, Bryan," he said, brushing the boy's head with his hand.

And then he was gone, leaving Dinah to wonder what had just happened. "Bryan, I think I'm going steady now," she said, sitting on the floor near her son.

"Gate."

"I think it's gate, too," she said with a chuckle as she rearranged the containers for him one more time.

Chapter Thirteen

Something had to be done about Priscilla and Payton. Now not only were they complaining to him about each other all the time, but they'd branched off and started to enlist help from other employees and board members as well.

Jeremy knew this because his dad, along with ten other people who should have had many more things to do, left the board meeting with nothing new to report but a "he said/she said" detailed report of the latest events of Payton and Priscilla's love life.

"Think I'm going to take a break from the club until all this is ironed over," his dad said to him with a sigh, which made Jeremy panic all the more.

If things didn't get settled down soon, no one would go to the club, Payton would start laying off workers, and Jeremy would be out of a pretty darn good temporary job.

Then he really wouldn't be able to get that house.

It was time for some drastic measures. "We need to talk," he announced, entering the kitchen just as Payton and Priscilla were about to launch into an quarrel centering on the merits of Texas, small Ohio towns, and the importance of honesty in relationships.

Priscilla looked fired up and ready to injure her boss within seconds.

Payton just looked bewildered and starstruck.

Enough was enough.

"We need to talk," he repeated a little more loudly. "Pull up some chairs."

Amazingly, they both did as he asked. "What's wrong?" Payton asked.

"You two."

"Me?" Priscilla said archly.

"You and Payton. I think it's high time the two of you stopped blaming the other person for imagined problems and started really listening to each other."

Payton frowned at his highhanded manner. "And tell me again why you are involved?"

Jeremy tried his best not to crack a smile. "Because you made me involved! You've been driving me crazy for a month, and now you've sought the advice of ten cranky board members."

"Hey, one of them is your father."

"I know every one of them very well, Payton. Just

as you do." He sighed, already dreading hearing his father complain about the atmosphere at the club. "Priscilla, eventually you will also know all these people very well. And, let me tell you . . . you *don't* want them involved in your personal life."

"I didn't ask them to be."

"I was merely soliciting their advice," Payton protested.

Priscilla scowled. "You were merely using your power and influence to veto my vote."

"Your idea was dumb."

"My idea was better than yours . . . which was idiotic."

Jeremy glanced from one to the other with a worried expression. If things didn't settle down soon, he'd have World War III on his hands. Sticking his thumb and pinky in his mouth, just like Kevin had taught him years ago, he blew fiercely.

Both Priscilla and Payton froze.

Payton looked impressed. "What are you doing?"

"Trying to gain some control of this situation. If you two would ask me—which you haven't, I might add— I think the reason you two are having such a difficult time working with each other is because there's something between you."

Both looked at him blankly. "You two obviously like each other," Jeremy finally stated.

"I do not!" Priscilla protested. "Honestly, Jeremy. Don't you have your own girl problems?"

"I do. And I'm trying to work them out. Maybe that's why I'm so in tune with yours."

"Thanks, but no thanks," Priscilla stated. "I've managed to live my life thus far without some wet-behind-the-ears college graduate tell me how to fall in love."

"Ah," Jeremy said, pleased.

"What?"

"You said, 'fall in love'."

Priscilla's green eyes narrowed. "I meant that in a generic way."

"Do you notice that Payton had been conspicuously silent so far?"

Both he and Priscilla turned to Payton, looking as cool as always across from them. Honestly, did the guy ever sweat? "I'm noticing now," Priscilla said. "What do you think about all this?"

"You might be surprised."

Her voice softened. "Why is that?"

Payton looked away. "Mainly because I think that part of what Jeremy is saying is exactly right."

She stared at him in shock. "Which part?"

"The part about feeling something for you."

Jeremy nudged him with his foot, practically stepping on it. "Say it. Tell her what you're thinking."

He sighed deeply. "When I first saw you in Houston, I was starstruck."

"Starstruck? I wasn't famous."

"How about lovestruck, then? That's the only way I can explain how I was feeling at that moment. The way people do when they see their idols in Hollywood. Breathless. Foolish. I saw you and I knew that we should be together."

"You've never said anything like that," Priscilla blurted, her expression incredulous.

"Because I knew you would say no. I knew if I came right out and told you I wanted to see you again, you'd tell me a dozen good reasons why we shouldn't."

"Well, yeah . . . we lived in different cities, we like different movies, music, and sports. You have this way about you that is always, eerily perfect, while I'm always a mess." Her voice drifted off. "I could go on for quite a while."

Payton raised an eyebrow. "See what I mean."

Jeremy leaned forward, bracing his elbows on his knees. "So you tricked her into coming to Ohio."

"Pretty much," Payton admitted. "I knew if I told you the club was really great, but about as far from as *nouveau*-trendy as McDonald's, you would turn me down flat."

Priscilla gasped in frustration. "But you said those things."

"And you believed me. Even after meeting Baron McKinley, who rhapsodized over the thought of having egg rolls on New Year's Day." He eyed her seriously. "I think there was a part of you that wanted a reason to come here, too."

Priscilla said nothing for a long minute. "You're

right, I guess. I was looking for something new . . . and I was attracted to you . . . and it just didn't make any sense. Things weren't supposed to happen that way."

"Like how?" Jeremy asked before the conversation got too out of hand. "What do you mean?"

"I mean that Payton, Ohio was everything my family said wasn't for me. They said I needed to live in the city, expand my resume, date men who were in the society pages, who were old school. I met Payton, then saw Payton, Ohio and realized I was just about to toss all my life-long plans away. I wasn't sure I could handle it." She sighed. "It was a whole lot easier to just blame Payton for my faults than face my insecurities."

"So you took it out on me?"

"You deserved some of it."

"I did."

Her gaze softened. "But, I did too."

Jeremy pursed his lips, uncomfortably aware of the many similarities their story had with his relationship with Dinah. Oh, sure . . . he hadn't lied to her. And Dinah wasn't the type of girl who would take out her revenge on him.

But, there was that feeling that she had snuck up on him, that they had snuck up on each other. He had instantly, completely known there was something about her that he never, ever wanted to give up.

Like Payton, he'd been willing to do whatever it

took to win her over. Life with Dinah wasn't the way he'd planned it would be. It wasn't how he'd planned to fall in love. And the timing wasn't terrific, either. But there was something there that was worth every sacrifice and tweaking of his former goals.

Because the alternative was unthinkable. He couldn't live without her. How could he, anyway? She was all he could think about.

"Jeremy?" Payton asked, his eyebrows raised.

"Huh? Oh, sorry," he said, realizing that he'd started daydreaming. He stood up. "Can I trust the two of you to be alone together and not do foolish things with big knives?" he asked, gesturing to the large set of knives displayed on the magnetic strip.

"You can," Priscilla said with a laugh. "Believe it or not, I think this is the first time that harming Payton is actually the furthest thing from my mind."

"Well, thank heaven for small favors," Payton said, stepping closer to her.

Feeling good about his match-making skills, Jeremy knew he was not needed any longer. "My job here is done. I'm going home."

"Got a car today?" Priscilla asked.

He laughed. "I do. Thanks for the offer, though."

And with that, he strode off, feeling better about pretty much everything.

"No ma'am. I don't have any books on gardening. This is pretty much only a fiction bookseller," Dinah replied to the elderly caller, trying to keep her voice as upbeat and positive as possible.

"Fiction?"

"Yep. All my books are pretend." She paused. "You might try the library, though. Or ask Mrs. Wexner down the way. She always has a beautiful garden."

The lady's voice brightened. "I know Marta Wexner."

Dinah smiled, pleased to have helped out in some way. "I feel certain she could help you figure out what's been eating your pansies."

"I think you're right."

"Yes, ma'am. Bye, now."

With a chuckle, Dinah hung up the phone. "If I had a dime for every person who wanted something that I don't have . . ."

"You'd have a small fortune, I image," Daphne Reece finished with a laugh.

Dinah chuckled, too, though she was terribly interested as to why Daphne had decided to pay her a visit that afternoon. During the two years she'd been open, Dinah couldn't ever recall the woman being a customer.

Her answer came right away. "I'm meeting Marianne McKinley here in a few minutes. She's going to show me that house Jeremy's interested in."

"Is Jeremy going, too?"

"No." Daphne picked up two of the newest best sellers, scanning the back covers. "He's at the club, then has a meeting at school with a few of the teachers in his department."

"He said that house is beautiful."

"From what Marianne told me, I don't think beautiful is quite the right adjective to use. But it is supposed to be unique." She gazed at Dinah, speculation in her eyes. "Just the type of place that needs some tender loving care."

"Sometimes those are the best kinds of places."

"I suppose you've never wanted to move out of your place."

Her comment took Dinah by surprise. "Actually, I probably would, if I ever got married again," she admitted. "My home has too many memories to start over in."

"It's been hard for you, huh?"

"Sometimes, sometimes not."

Daphne looked uncertainly at the door, then as if she made up her mind, stepped forward. "When Jeremy first told me about you, he wore an expression I'd only seen on my kids' faces just weeks before they got engaged."

Dinah didn't know what to say to that.

"And, I have to tell you . . . at first I wasn't too thrilled about seeing my youngest son so ready to grow up and get married."

Thinking of Bryan, Dinah said, "I guess I can imagine that feeling."

"But after seeing you and him together, I realize I was wrong."

"Mrs. Reece, I don't know if we're quite at the place where you're imagining."

"I know that. I guess I just wanted you to know that if you and Jeremy ever do decide to become more serious, you two have my blessing." She glanced out the window again. "Ah, here's Marianne. We'll stop by afterwards and tell you more about that house."

And before Dinah could even raise a hand to wave her off, Daphne was scampering down the front steps of her store, her high-heeled sandals clicking as she went.

Dinah watched her leave, then sat down for a moment, pleased when Bonnie woke up from her nap long enough to walk over to be petted.

"I guess I do need to make some decisions, huh, Bonnie?" she asked, rubbing the dog's long soft ears. "All this time I've been content with my life, content to just live . . . not get too emotionally involved. Afraid to get hurt again."

Bonnie glanced up, her velvet brown eyes softening in what seemed to be understanding. Dinah pressed a kiss to the top of her nose. "But that's not really fair to anyone, is it?"

She thought of Bryan, of her parents . . . of Jeremy. Each was there for her. She only needed to decide how much she was willing to give to Jeremy. Was she ready to love again? To maybe get hurt?

With the way her body felt like jelly every time she was near Jeremy, Dinah had a feeling that she already had her answer.

She already was falling in love again . . . and it didn't matter whether she thought she was ready or not.

Chapter Fourteen

"Hey, Stratton, Joanne," Jeremy said as his sister and brother-in-law entered the kitchen. "Now, why am I not surprised y'all are joining us for dinner?"

Joanne raised an eyebrow. "I don't know, since the whole family is here."

"Did you really think anyone was going to skip this dinner?" Stratton asked with a half-smirk. "No way was anyone going to pass up the opportunity to watch your parents grill you and Dinah. Joanne canceled her plans to go to the movies to be here."

"I'm honored," Jeremy said, glancing at his sister with more than a little bit of wariness. "You're not going to do anything weird, are you?"

"Like what?"

"I don't know."

"I like Dinah," she said then bent over and kissed his forehead. "I like my little brother, too. Don't worry."

"Don't do that."

"Don't do what? Kiss your head? I've been doing that since you were a baby."

"Don't call me little brother. I'm taller than you."

"Jeremy—" she began, then grunted as her husband stepped on her toe.

"Gosh, I'm sorry, Jo. I sure didn't mean to interrupt." He grabbed her arm. "Let's go look in the kitchen to make sure everything is okay," Stratton said, deftly moving Joanne out of the living room.

Missy glanced up at Jeremy with a smile. "Everything's going to be just fine, you know."

Drawn closer by her comforting voice and sweet disposition, Jeremy sat down on the couch next to her. "I just don't want Dinah to get overwhelmed by everyone. You know how they can be."

"I know how fun and caring your family can be. Let Dinah handle it. She'll do just fine."

"You mean because she's older?"

Missy shook her head in exasperation. "No, I mean because she's great with people." Just as his parents and Kevin walked out of the kitchen she whispered, "Worrying about what makes you two different is going to tear you up inside. Just concentrate on how you're alike."

The doorbell rang before he had a chance to think of a suitable reply.

"I'll get it," Jim called out. "Can't wait to get my hands on Bryan."

He opened the door, and with a booming 'hello', he picked up a bewildered Bryan and ushered Dinah into the living room. "Look who's here," Jim announced to the room unnecessarily. "Bryan."

"And Dinah," Jeremy said with a smile as he took the plate of cookies she'd brought with her.

Everyone crowded around both Dinah and Bryan, oohing and ahhing over Bryan's shiny new tiny tooth. "How are you?" he asked her once they got a break.

"Just fine."

"I was worried, after today, you might not come."

"I've been planning on it all day long."

"You'll get her later, dear," Daphne told her son as she grasped Dinah's arm. "Right now I'm taking Dinah into the kitchen. We need to catch up."

He wasn't aware they'd ever said more than the barest greetings in passing. But as he watched her go, he couldn't help but feel proud of how great she looked, and at how naturally she fit in.

A brief knock rang out before the front door opened again, this time bringing in Mary Beth, Cameron, and Maggie.

Jeremy shook his head. Could his parents ever have just one or two of their children over at a time? Could any of his siblings ever pass up a chance to be part of the mass confusion? He pretty much doubted it.

"How're you doing?" Cameron asked after everyone got settled.

"Okay, I guess. Mom has Dinah cornered in the kitchen."

"Dinah has Bryan on her side. Trust me, Dinah will be able to do no wrong."

Jeremy chuckled at that. Slowly, as usual, everyone staffed their favorite stations, and dinner was prepared. Jim, Stratton, and Kevin manned the grill and talked baseball; Mary Beth and Missy set the table and organized the buffet. Dinah paired with Daphne and made the salad and rolls, and Jeremy, Cameron, and Joanne watched the two kids.

Finally everything was ready. And, in time honored tradition, Jim put their guest at the front of the line. "Dinah, lead us on through," he boomed, like they were marching into battle.

Jeremy bit back a smile as Dinah gave him a little salute before picking up a paper plate. He'd watched her often during the first half hour she'd been there, and it looked as if she was doing just fine. More than once she and his mom had been in deep conversation, or she'd been laughing with his dad.

He went through the line himself, grabbed a cheeseburger and some coleslaw for himself, then took a seat next to Dinah. Bryan was happily gnawing on a cold carrot, having eaten some baby food while the burgers were still cooking.

"What do you think?" he asked as soon as they were both settled.

"I'm having a great time."

Great sounded a little excessive. "Really? No one's driving you crazy?"

Her dimple popped. "Just you."

His plate almost slipped off his lap. "Why do you say that?"

"I've hardly seen you."

Once again he felt a twinge of satisfaction. "I'll stay by your side from now on."

Her brown eyes danced.

"Tell us about Beagle's Books, Dinah," his mom said from across the table.

"All right." Within minutes, everyone was in discussion again, this time about running a business, books in general, and finding good help. This led to a brief analysis of types of pets, and finally to raising children.

"I don't know how you've done it," Mary Beth said frankly. "Cam and I have each other and both our families, and we still get overwhelmed."

Dinah shrugged. "I got lucky. Bryan's a pretty easy guy. He sleeps well, and is a great fan of Tupperware."

Mary Beth grinned. "That helps, but I think you have more to do with his happy, easy going demeanor than you're letting on. Are you really organized?"

Dinah shrugged. "I suppose." Her face became more serious. "I'm not going to lie to you. There's been more than one day when I've felt like throwing up my hands in frustration. Or just wishing I could go take a one hour nap. It's not easy."

Bryan crawled over to Jeremy and held his hands up. Jeremy reached down and pulled him into his lap, feeling almost every eye on him.

"Well, now you've got Jeremy," Daphne announced, with a proud maternal smile.

Jeremy felt like sliding right down into the down of the couch. But Dinah only looked amused. "Now, I do, thank goodness," she said.

Like magic, the band of tension around his lungs evaporated. With a few words, Dinah had just cemented their relationship. Now he had to figure out what to do next.

"Would you like to go for a walk?" he asked her. "I'm sure everyone could watch Bryan for a bit, if he doesn't mind."

Dinah glanced at her son. He'd just crawled to Daphne and was currently fascinated with Daphne's necklace, with its wide array of brightly painted enamel charms hanging from it. "I think Bryan will be just fine . . . if you think you can handle him, Mrs. Reese."

"It's Daphne, and I know I can," she said. "You two go, now. We'll just get ready for dessert while you're gone."

That seemed to be all he needed to hear. Like a shot, Jeremy was standing, reaching for her hand, and with a small wave, led her out of the crowded room.

As soon as they stood outside on the front stoop, he let out a relieved sigh. "You okay?"

She wondered what he was referring to. . . . the huge meal, the experience of being on a date with a half-dozen chaperones, or her feelings after the questioning. But no matter what the reference, her answer was the same. "I am."

He took her hand, led her down the street. "I can honestly tell you that I didn't think this gathering would be quite so big, though I'm not sure why I thought that."

"I don't mind. I'm close to my brothers, too. I just don't get to see them very often. And your parents remind me a lot of mine." She gazed at him, willing him to understand how she was feeling. "It really is nice to be around other families that get along so well."

"I suppose."

As they walked a little farther, he pointed out some of the history of different houses, then they fell silent, merely enjoying each other's company. "How are those costumes coming along?"

"Fine. They're almost done. I'm having a good time sewing them."

"I don't know how you even have time to sew them."

"It's been almost two months since Joanne first approached me. I've scheduled them in."

He rolled his eyes. "Every time I see you, you've got a schedule for the day."

"Some would say you're not that different."

He laughed. "I guess not."

He thought of a thousand things they could talk about: the club, a meeting he'd had at the high school about schedules and Special Ed students. The new book he was reading. The house on Maple that he couldn't stop driving by. But none of that seemed very interesting at all. Not compared to what was at the forefront of his mind. "I want to kiss you again," he blurted, then cursed himself for stating it so clumsily.

Her dimple appeared. "I was hoping you would."

He leaned forward, smelled her fresh, clean scent. Liked the way her breath hitched, like this time alone meant just as much to her as to him. "Really?"

"Positively."

Finally their lips met. "I'm glad you came over, Dinah," he said, wrapping his arms around her and holding her close.

She smiled brightly. "I am, too. Jeremy?"

"Yeah?"

"Just kiss me, would you?"

He touched his lips to hers, not even needing to hear her ask again. Ah, she was so sweet.

Chapter Fifteen

Time was running out. Three weeks had gone by, school was going to be starting soon, and Jeremy knew he had to make a decision about the house soon. Marianne McKinley called yesterday with news that there'd been quite a few other showings during the last week, and one couple seemed pretty serious. Jeremy couldn't explain exactly why, but he wanted to live in that house on Maple, and he wanted to live there sooner than later.

It struck him as strange and foreign, this sudden need to have things immediately. He'd always been the kind of person to bide his time, to wait for the right moment. He'd rarely been impulsive, rarely done things when he wasn't absolutely certain the time was right. His impatient needs were driving him crazy.

Once more, he studied the paperwork in front of him, the neatly organized bank statements, financial records; the copy of his new school contract. How was he going to make everything work out? He wanted that house, but, if he was honest with himself, he also really wanted a home for himself and Dinah. Not her house; Neil and she had bought that together. It was part of her history, not theirs. And he was enough of a man to realize that he would have a hard time moving his things into another man's closet. Even under the circumstances, such as they were.

He leaned back against his chair. Who was he fooling, anyway? Dinah would probably laugh if he asked her to marry him. And be appalled if he said that his dream was to move her and Bryan out of their snug little house into a sprawling old place in need of months, not weeks of work.

As he processed what he'd just thought, his thoughts caught him off guard. When had that happened? When had he decided that he wanted to marry her? All along, his conscious told him. From the moment he'd spied Dinah hand Bryan a camel cookie, he'd fallen hard for her.

It had just taken almost three months for the rest of him to catch up to his heart.

Luckily the phone rang and got him out of his mood. "Hello?"

"Jeremy? Oh, thank goodness," Dinah exclaimed. "I need your help."

"What's wrong?" Her voice was panicked, sounding as if she was on the verge of tears. "Honey, what's happened?"

"It's Bryan," she said, her tone rising two octaves. "His finger . . . his finger got slammed in a door. He's crying; it's bleeding. I think it's broken."

A sudden, fierce panic rose in him. "I'll be right there," he said, the angry howls of Bryan in the background making his stomach clench.

"Really? Are you sure? My mom's not around, and I can't take him to the hospital by myself."

"I'm on my way, honey. Two minutes."

He hung up before hearing her reply, and was pulling open the back door within minutes.

"What's wrong?" his mom called out to him.

"Bryan's hurt. Dinah and I need to take him to the hospital," he called out.

"Oh, no! Do you want me to come, too?"

"No. We've got it," he said as he lowered himself into his sports car. "I've got my cell. I'll let you know what's going on later."

As soon as he arrived at Dinah's, she greeted him at the door, Bryan cradled in her arms. Straight away, he gazed at Bryan. He was crying loud enough to beat the band, and Dinah had tears of her own streaming down her cheeks. "I don't know what happened," she said tearfully. "I think a gust of wind blew a door shut."

"It was an accident, Dinah. They happen." Carefully, he brushed his lips against her brow. "Let's go." As best he could, he guided her to her car, where they buckled a screaming Bryan into a car seat. "I'll drive. You sit back there." He paused, trying to stay calm. "Have you called the doctor?"

"No, it's Sunday . . ." She shook her head. "I just panicked."

Jeremy quickly dialed Stratton's mobile phone number, glad it was on the directory of his cell phone. As he pulled out of her driveway, he handed her the phone. "Talk to Stratton," he said. "He'll know what to do."

In a daze, she did as she was told, and by the time he made the way to the first stop sign, Dinah was speaking quietly to Stratton, answering a series of questions.

"Should we still go to the hospital?" he called out.

"Yes," she said, looking up from a still weepy Bryan. "Stratton thinks he'll need x-rays."

"Okay." As best he could, he raced to the hospital, then guided Dinah and Bryan into the emergency doors. As he helped Dinah get checked in, he saw Stratton enter the double doors.

"What are you doing here?" he asked his brother-in-law. It wasn't usual for Stratton to give up his Sunday afternoons for non-emergencies.

Stratton shrugged. "I had a few minutes."

With Stratton's help, they were rushed through the preliminary paper work, and within minutes both

Stratton and an emergency room doctor were unwrapping Bryan's hand from a blood-soaked towel and bag of ice.

Jeremy winced as he caught hold of the little boy's chubby hand. His nail bed was already black and blue, and swollen at least two times its normal size.

Dinah's lip was red and puffy as well, and with a tug in his heart, he realized that she'd been biting her lip to stay in control. The sight made him want to pull her into his arms and hold her tight. How many times had she done such a thing, all by herself? How many times had she chewed her lip raw in order to stay in control, to do what was right for Bryan?

When did Dinah fall apart, ask for help? And more importantly, had anyone ever been there to catch her when she did?

"We'll need to go down to x-rays," Stratton directed. "Once those are completed, we'll know more."

She nodded silently, her brown eyes settling on Stratton with absolute trust. Together, the four of them went to the x-ray room, and Jeremy watched Dinah cry silent tears as she held Bryan down so they could get their x-rays.

Later, after ascertaining that his finger was only bruised, not broken, they bandaged Bryan's whole fist up, so it looked as if he wore a little club.

And because Dinah looked exhausted, Jeremy stepped forward and listened to the majority of the directions for care and follow up appointments.

Less than two hours after they had arrived at Memorial Hospital, they were leaving again. "I can't thank you enough for meeting us here," Dinah said to Stratton as they walked to the car, Bryan now sound asleep in her arms.

Stratton brushed a stray curl from Bryan's forehead. "I'm just glad you called."

She glanced at Jeremy. "It was Jeremy's idea. I was so frightened."

Stratton smiled at her and squeezed her arm. "You are a good mom. I would have been worried if you hadn't been worried."

She chuckled at that. "I must be a great mom, then."

"See you two later. Call me at home if you need anything, Dinah. I mean it."

"I will," she said, turning to Jeremy as he unlocked her car doors. "I hardly even remember getting here," she said in surprise.

Jeremy glanced at her and once again wanted to hold her close. "It's been quite an afternoon. Come on, we'll get you two home."

He drove them to her house, then helped her settle the still-sleeping Bryan in his bed. Then he finally did what he'd been dying to do from the moment he'd heard her frightened voice.

"Come here," he said, leading her to the couch.

When she followed him easily, he sat down, and pulled her onto his lap. She settled in.

"I've been wanting to hold you since the moment I saw your poor chewed-up lip. Let me do this."

Her fingers covered her mouth. "My lips?" Her eyes widened as she finally noticed her raw mouth. "Oh my gosh. What a mess I am."

"Not at all," he murmured. "You're just fine. Sit here for a moment, then I'll make you some iced tea."

Finally, she relaxed against him, and right then and there he knew he was a goner. He loved them both. He wanted Dinah in his life forever, and Bryan, too. All he had to do was figure out a way to make her believe that he was worth it.

"Poor Bryan," Dinah's mother cooed a few hours later as she knelt on the floor next to him.

He glanced up at her and smiled, then went back to his trusty pile of measuring cups and plastic plates. Miraculously, Bryan seemed to be recovering from his little experience much easier than Dinah could have ever imagined.

As soon as he'd woken up, he'd squirmed from her arms and insisted on playing with his toys right next to Bonnie, his bandaged hand hardly slowing him down. Dinah wished she felt as perky.

"What a day you've had," her mom said, looking over Bryan's head to Dinah.

She couldn't help but agree. It had been quite a day. "I'm in no hurry to make another trip to the emergency room any time soon."

"He's twenty-six months and already made a trip. This doesn't bode well."

"He's a boy. That's what boys do," her father quipped.

Like that was supposed to make her feel any better. "I hope he gives me at least a year or two before we make another trip," Dinah said, compromising. "He may be all boy, but I'm just a mere woman."

Her mom laughed. "You did just fine, honey. You always do."

Did she? There was a big part of her that didn't think so. And a whole other portion of her that was tired of handling crises alone. It had felt really good to have Jeremy there, calling Stratton, talking to the doctors and nurses, and holding her after everything was okay. "Jeremy helped a lot," she said, feeling the need to give credit where credit was due.

Her parents exchanged glances. "We heard. Daphne called us on the golf course and relayed how Jeremy was on his feet and out the door only seconds after you called." She gave Dinah a sideways glance. "He must really care for you."

Their quiet, assessing glances made heat rise to her cheeks, which made her feel even more self-conscious. How come at almost thirty years of age, she still felt perpetually fourteen around her mom? Especially when her mom gave her those assessing glances? "I guess he does," she replied, mainly just to see what her parents said to that.

"I like him, too," her dad boomed. "Like his parents, his sisters, that Stratton. You could do worse, dear."

She bristled at his words. Gosh, her dad was making her sound like some sort of old maid! "I was married before, remember?"

"We liked Neil, too," her mom said, eager to play mediator. "It's just that . . . well, he's gone, honey."

She knew that all too well. "I don't think I need to be in a hurry to do anything."

"We wouldn't want you to. Though, I would hate your feelings about Neil to interfere with any thoughts you might have of being with Jeremy."

"I loved Neil."

"We did, too."

"He was a good husband. A good father," she pointed out, feeling the need to defend him though the things they were saying out loud were nothing she hadn't thought to herself before.

Her father nodded, his expression solemn. "Yes, he was."

Dinah slumped. "Then why am I so afraid to fall in love again?"

Her parents looked at each other in alarm, but for once Dinah was tired of hiding her feelings behind a sunny smile. "I had a good marriage with Neil. I wanted him to settle down, wanted him to want to be with me . . ."

"You had a good marriage with him. He was a good

man. He also hardly thought of the future, had to go out with his buddies once a weekend, and had a need-less accident while you were home with his baby."

"Dad!"

"I'm sorry, but I don't understand how we have to make him out to be a saint when he was nothing of the sort," he said, defending himself. "I thought Neil was a great guy . . . but he had faults. Just like you and I do."

Her father stood up as if to prove his point. "He was human. And he was speeding in the rain because he liked fast cars and danger. The police reports proved it."

She really didn't want to revisit those feelings. "I don't know why we have to bring this up right now."

Her mother marched forward, her auburn hair bouncing from the motion. "Maybe because we never do. Maybe it's time to actually talk about things in-stead of pretending they don't matter. All I've ever heard you say about Jeremy Reece is what's wrong with him. 'He's too young. He should be with some-one else. He's just starting out'." Her expression soft-ened. "But maybe, just maybe you're so busy looking at all the reasons you shouldn't be together instead of all the reasons you should."

It was nothing new to have her mother give her relationship advice . . . but completely weird to actu-ally find herself listening to it. "What do you mean?"

"I mean Jeremy was there for you today, and he

seems like the kind of guy who's going to be there for you all the time."

Dinah knew that.

"And, I imagine, you would be there for him . . . right?"

With a start, Dinah knew that exactly. If their places had been reversed, if he'd called her in a panic, she would have dropped everything to be with him. That's what love was.

Stunned by her revelation, she hardly heard her mother drone on. ". . . he's dependable, likeable, cute as can be, and shoot, the whole school board thinks he's about as great as sliced bread."

That brought her up short. "Sliced bread?" she echoed with a smile.

Her mother rolled her eyes. "You know what I mean. I think you should take a step back and do some thinking, Dinah. Or you're going to miss out on a great guy."

And with that, her parents took off, leaving Dinah with a messy kitchen, a sleepy Bryan, and a whole lot to think about.

Chapter Sixteen

"**M**y turn for the fitting," Missy announced, walking into the back of Beagle's Books. "Thanks for letting me come here to try on the dress instead of going to your house. It's so nice to take care of this during my lunch hour."

"I'm happy to do it," Dinah said, handing Missy a vibrant scarlet colored dress.

"Red?"

"You're going to look beautiful in it. Besides, Joanne said the red fabric was on sale."

"I bet an ivory color was on sale, too," Missy grumbled, heading to the rest room. "Joanne just has a flair for the dramatic. I'll be out in a sec."

Moments later Missy appeared, looking resplendent in red. "I like that color on you," Dinah said.

"Me, too . . . if you want to know the truth."

Dinah was relieved to see that she didn't have too many more alterations. Basically, all that needed to be done was just a little pinning around the shoulders and the hemming.

"Are you excited about the baby?"

Missy's eyes glowed. "So excited. Sometimes Kevin and I can hardly believe that we're going to be parents soon."

"When's your due date, again?"

"Around Christmas."

Dinah did some quick calculations. "The baby will be sitting up and crawling this summer."

Missy glanced at her, wide-eyed. "Gosh, you're right! It's hard to believe how different things will be . . . just one year from now." She glanced at herself in the mirror, turning this way and that, before directing her attention back to Dinah. "Did you know this is my second marriage?"

"I'd heard that."

"My first was pretty tough. We only lasted ten months. I was sure before I met Kevin that I was going to be alone for the rest of my life. Isn't it funny how love can find you when you're not looking for it?"

Thinking back to her trip to the grocery store, Dinah nodded. "It is funny."

"I think you and Jeremy are adorable together."

"Thank you."

"How's Bryan's hand doing?"

"Better," Dinah said with relief. "My mom has him today. I think I'm more traumatized than he was. I was so scared when he was hurt."

"I'll bet. I heard Jeremy was worried sick over the both of you."

The revelation that Jeremy cared enough to worry made her feel good inside. "Really?"

"Really." She spun, looking into the mirror from all angles as her dress billowed out around her ankles. "Well, I guess this will do. Sure you don't want to change your mind about participating in the reenactment?"

"Positive," Dinah replied. "Bryan and I will stand on the sidelines and ooh and aah at all the action."

"Smart girl."

Dinah chuckled. With the reenactment just days away, she wasn't sure how smart she was feeling. Constantly she found herself forgetting things, zoning out people, gazing outside . . . thinking about Jeremy.

She felt in love, that all encompassing feeling she'd used to feel with Neil. But this time, it felt richer, more multi-faceted. She felt giddy, excited, nervous, and unsure . . . all at the same time whenever he was near!

Yep, falling in love with Jeremy Reece might not be the easiest thing she had ever done . . . but it certainly did make her feel like she had stepped back into the land of the living.

* * *

Hours later, just as she was closing up, Jeremy stopped by. "Thought I'd take you out for an ice cream," he said, leaning on her counter.

Her heart lurched, and she felt that now familiar splurge of emotions as she caught his scent. "That's nice," she murmured, ready to do anything with him.

Then reality set in. Her mom had had Bryan all day and was probably going crazy. "Not tonight," she said with genuine regret. "Bryan—"

"Is with your mom and excited about her two new boxes of kitchen containers," he finished, humor lighting his eyes. "Come on, even working girls need a treat sometimes." He took her hand and guided her around the counter. "I've been looking forward to seeing you all afternoon. You're not going to disappoint me, are you?"

What could she say to that? She'd missed him, too. "No," she said, enjoying the feel of her hand in his. "I'm not about to disappoint you." She smiled at him then. "Thank you for coming to get me. An ice cream sounds like heaven."

He took her hand as soon as she locked up and guided her down the hill to downtown Payton, the little two block intersection that was composed of The Mill, the Payton Grill, and several cute antique and gift shops. Catty-corner to it all was an old-fashioned ice cream parlor.

They held hands as they walked, filling each other in on their days. Dinah enjoyed the sight of him next to her . . . and found herself dreaming of a future of ice cream visits, walks through town, special glances at each other that meant so much.

She chose a double dip of chocolate chip and grinned when Jeremy chose plain vanilla. "Nothing more exciting for you?"

"I don't need exciting ice cream, I've got you," he said gallantly.

She smiled at his joke. "Thank you very much."

Then they held hands and walked up and down the sidewalks, staring into windows and talking about nothing. More than a few people stopped and said 'hi', and one gentleman even said that they looked just like high school sweethearts.

With some surprise, Dinah realized that that was exactly how she did feel, and she thought it was wonderful. Feeling giddy, she leaned close and kissed him.

He glanced at her in surprise. "What was that for?"

"For being you."

"What? Just because I take you out for ice cream on a Thursday night?"

"Yes. And because you think of me. And you hold my hand." She breathed deeply, gathering her courage. "I like being with you, Jeremy. You make me feel good inside."

His cheeks colored. Then, out of the blue, he leaned over and kissed her again, this time a little more pas-

Chapter Seventeen

Finally, the big day had come. Dinah grinned broadly as she watched Jeremy stride toward her front porch.

"Might I offer you an escort to the reenactment, ma'am?" Jeremy called out as he approached.

She had to laugh. He looked very gallant in his navy blue uniform with rows of gold braid. Good enough for her to forget just how tricky that gold braid had been to secure.

"I'd be delighted," she replied. "You look very handsome."

"Thank you," he said, bowing slightly. "My seamstress has a way with a needle . . . and other things."

She blushed, thinking of the kisses they'd recently

shared. And the ones she was looking forward to. "I'd say you were a lucky man, then."

He picked her up and twirled her around, much to the amusement of Bryan and Bonnie. "Yes, I am."

Her body tingled from their brief contact and she swallowed hard after he set her back down. "Are you ready?" she asked.

"Ready as I'll ever be."

Quickly they let Bonnie inside, then secured Bryan in his stroller, Jeremy talking to him the whole time about his day. Finally, Dinah picked up her picnic basket, handed Jeremy a large thermos of cold water, and they were on their way. "I brought my camera; I'll take lots of pictures."

"Take them quick, I'm supposed to 'die' early."

She chuckled. "How does the jacket feel?"

"It feels great, just warm. Wearing this really makes me feel for the soldiers. The pants and jacket don't breathe much."

"So, it's only supposed to be ninety-two degrees today. Good thing Joanne read somewhere that it was perfectly acceptable to reenact in the morning."

Jeremy grunted, already pulling at the long sleeves of his jacket. "Good thing she listened to all the men who threatened not to show up if she staged it at two in the afternoon."

"I've brought my video camera," she said. "I'll take lots of pictures."

"Thanks. I was actually thinking that this experience

would come in handy at school. We study the War Between the States during second quarter."

"That's the War of Northern Aggression, I believe."

"Ah, spoken like a true Southerner."

She chuckled, and for the next half hour they enjoyed the novelty of seeing various "soldiers" appearing out of houses and walking to the park together. Here and there women appeared, looking resplendent in hooped skirts the colors of sherbets.

Jeremy smiled at the sight of a ten-year-old boy racing one of his friends down the sidewalk, all dressed up in short pants and a drum. "It's times like this when I really appreciate my sister Joanne. This will be an event that will have people talking for the next couple of years."

"I imagine you're right," she said, knowing she would recall the day for years to come, too . . . and not because of any historical significance. She loved walking next to him, being with him, doing things with him. She felt proud to be by his side.

Suddenly, it didn't matter what anyone else thought about their differences in ages or experiences. All Dinah knew was that Jeremy was one of the nicest men she'd ever met; he was great to be around; he curled her toes when he kissed her, and . . . he just happened to look great in a Union uniform.

They walked on, waving to more friends, when Dinah realized just where they were. "Hey, look at your house!" she exclaimed. Someone had planted row after row of begonias in the front yard. Their red and pink blooms looked vibrant and pretty, setting off the stone-work of the historical home. "Whoever hired the land-scaper didn't pay him enough. It looks amazing."

"It does look beautiful, but it's not mine yet."

Glancing at him, she noticed the worry in his eyes and strived to make him feel better. On the spur of the moment, she steered the stroller up the front path. "I do think you should go ahead and get it, Jeremy," Dinah said, stepping up on the empty front porch. "It's a peach of a place."

He chuckled at the phrase but had to agree. It was a peach of a place. And, because he was in no hurry to go pretend to either shoot someone or play dead, he decided the time was just as good as any to admit the truth. "It's great . . . though I have to tell you that the price of the house isn't the only thing I've been saving up for."

"What else?"

He looked into her eyes, saw sympathy and friend-ship, and realized she probably had no idea just how much he loved her. "I love you, Dinah," he said baldly, steeling himself for her surprise, yet knowing he couldn't tell her his dreams without explaining his motivations first. "I haven't wanted to rush you, but over these last three months, I've really come to care for you, deeply."

Finally, he steeled himself to meet her gaze. But all

he saw was love shining in her eyes. "I love you, too," she said simply.

He shook his head in wonder, then did the only thing that seemed appropriate: he pulled her into his arms and held her close, kissing her cheeks and neck, then finally her lips. "I'm so glad. See, I've been hoping to one day ask you to marry me."

He held his breath. There. It was said.

Her eyes widened. "Marry?"

Jeremy nodded. "Yeah. I feel so stupid, telling you this in a ridiculously hot Union uniform. But, I don't want to live here without you and Bryan. I don't want to think about a future without the two of you in it."

"I don't know what to say."

"You don't have to say a word," he replied, sure her mind must be reeling. "Just think about it. By the time I save up enough money for us to get married, maybe you'll have made up your mind," he said with a smile.

She chewed her lip. "I want a future with you in it, too, but I don't understand why you think you have to have a home and a large savings account in order for us to make it work."

He glanced at Dinah. She looked confused and more than a little irritated. Now he felt really silly. "Because I want to provide for you, Dinah. I want to take care of you."

She stepped back. "I think your costume has addled your mind."

Now he was thoroughly confused. "What's wrong? Are you upset that I told you I wanted to marry you?"

"No. I'm upset that you thought conditions had to be perfect in order for us to do so." She ran her fingers through her hair, making the flipped ends curl up even more. "Jeremy, I don't need all those things. I don't need to be taken care of. I already have a home, a business . . . a life."

And he, obviously, didn't have any of those things. And, though she was telling him she didn't expect him to have a home and a full time job, he felt their absence even more. "I know that."

"I don't need you to provide them for me."

Dinah's voice was clipped, almost hard, and her lack of understanding made him lose his temper. "Maybe you don't need money or a home, but you do need a husband, someone to love you," he pointed out angrily. "You need someone who will accept you no matter what, who will be there for you through thick and thin. And Bryan . . . he needs a father. Someone who wants to be with him, to take him to the hospital when he gets hurt. To play with him in the sandbox, to hold him when he's sleepy. He needs me, and so do you," he finished softly.

Dinah's eyes filled with tears. "Jeremy, that isn't what I meant, you misunderstood me."

He shook his head. "No, Dinah, you've misunderstood me. Everything I've done all summer was with you and Bryan in mind. I don't need you to want to trip over yourself in a rush to marry me, but I do want you to take me seriously."

"I do," she said softly.

"Do you?" He gripped the front porch banister tightly, doing his best to school his emotions so he wouldn't do something else stupid and start explaining himself again.

"Then why do I have to keep explaining myself? Why do you hold me at a distance? Why are you denying something that could be so beautiful between us?" He sighed, a gurgle from Bryan making him realize that this was not the place to have an argument. Not on the front porch in front of Bryan. "I better get going."

"Jeremy . . ."

"I'll see you later," he said, over his shoulder, more than ready to get out of her way. His pace quickened, and seeing several guys he knew from high school, he joined them, letting them give him grief over being in the production.

For the first time, he was actually glad he was about to pretend he was in a battle. At least then he could vent off some of his anger.

Dinah fought back tears as she watched Jeremy storm away. She'd meant every word she'd said, but she hadn't meant to state it like that. And she really hadn't meant to blurt out everything without time to explain why she said those things.

But instead of getting him to understand her motivations, she'd run him off. She glanced at Bryan, and with a feeling of surprise, she realized he'd fallen asleep. With a sigh, she sat on the old wooden porch beside him, leaning her back against the cool wood.

He'd talked about wanting to marry her and Bryan, of her needing someone to love; of Bryan needing a father. But did he need her just as much?

She had a feeling he did.

She thought again of all the things he'd said. He wanted to provide for her. To take care of her. All of those goals were noble, indeed.

She wanted a marriage, a different one than she'd had with Neil. She wanted one in which she felt like an equal partner. One in which she could face problems and crises with a friend, a lover. With someone who was certain to be by her side for years to come.

She wanted Jeremy. She loved him. With a start, she realized that she'd loved him for quite some time, now. But how could she show him?

More soldiers walked by, along with more than one lady in full regalia. She waved to a few, told a man she'd hope he'd survive the battle, chuckled at the sight of a pair of moms armed with oversized beach bags, picnic baskets, and a small army of children to watch.

And then Marianne McKinley walked by and Dinah knew she'd just found her answer. "Mrs. McKinley, could I speak with you for a moment?" she asked, jumping to her feet.

Mrs. McKinley approached. "Hey, Dinah. What are you doing here?"

"I've been doing some serious thinking, and I need your help."

"You going to the reenactment?"

"I was, but I was kind of hoping that I could take advantage of the empty streets and do something first."

"I'm game. What's on your mind?"

"I have quite a bit of money saved up, and I was hoping that perhaps you could help me help buy a house."

Marianne's eyes practically glowed. "This sounds better than any old reenactment . . . ah, don't tell Joanne I said that."

"I won't, if you won't tell Joanne that I feel the same way." She stepped down the stairs. "Here's my plan," she began, enlisting Mrs. McKinley's aid in her own battle to win Jeremy's heart.

Chapter Eighteen

Lying on the wet grass, pretending to be dead, and ignoring the sounds of a fierce battle raging around him, all gave Jeremy a lot of time to reflect on many things. First off, he thought it would have probably been a good idea to tell the city not to water the grass just an hour before a hundred men were about to lie down on it.

Next, Joanne really needed to go on a vacation. She was stressed, irritable, and was sporting a nasty cut from a not-quite-plastic saber. She was also driving everyone crazy. He needed to discuss with Stratton the benefits a Mediterranean Cruise would have for his wife. Perhaps planning a trip to somewhere far away would give her something else to do besides organize historical activities.

And last, but not least, Jeremy knew he needed to find Dinah and apologize to her. He'd taken every word she'd said, added his own unhealthy mix of insecurities to it, and pretty much ruined whatever chance he'd had with her.

And he managed to do it while looking like a geek. That was the final straw.

Two cameramen approached. Jeremy closed his eyes and did his best to remain completely still and lifeless. He had to admit that the fake blood along his thigh did look pretty real and repulsive. It was going to look awesome on tape.

Thirty more minutes passed, then with a loud pop from a cap gun, the reenactment was over. People clapped, bowed, clasped hands, and groaned from muscles being cramped in one position for too long.

As usual, his family had planned a party to celebrate the occasion. Before he'd messed everything up with Dinah and Bryan, the three of them had intended to attend.

Deciding to skip out before any member of his family could either ask him where Dinah and Bryan were, or subject him to a thousand questions, Jeremy quickly picked up his canteen, hat, and wooden rifle, and walked towards the walking path near the river. He would just have to follow the path, cut through the back of the country club, and then he'd practically be at the house where they'd fought.

Quickly he strode off, keeping his head down so no

one would recognize him. He maneuvered around a pair of boys fishing in the river, between two bike riders on the path, then approached the back of the country club, the greens looking curiously empty.

But then something caught his eye. Two figures doing an activity very different than golfing! As he approached, he saw it was none other than Payton and Priscilla, kissing like there was no tomorrow. "Hey," he called out, just because he was feeling ornery and they'd caused him so much grief.

Payton looked up from Priscilla's face with a scowl, then grinned as he recognized Jeremy. "Hey. How was the battle?"

"Died in the first round of fire."

"Too bad."

"Yeah. Grass was soaked."

Priscilla pointed toward his leg. "Great looking injury."

"Thanks." He gestured to the two of them. "The two of you look pretty great together, if you don't mind me saying so."

Both Payton and Priscilla burst into wide smiles. "Thanks!" Priscilla called out. "Once we stopped arguing, we figured there was a lot of things keeping us together."

"Have I thanked you for your help?" Payton asked.

"Nope."

"Thanks!"

"No problem. By the way, I need the day off today."

"You got it."

With a wave, Jeremy strode on, the couple hardly noticing he'd left them.

At last, he reached the top of a small hill, and started his descent toward Dinah. He hoped she'd be home. They had a lot to discuss, and he had some groveling to do, as well.

He walked on, feeling mildly uncomfortable in the damp wool. As he unbuttoned the first two buttons, he decided to make a slight detour and walk by his dream house. It was time to once and for all forget about that place. He had other things to concentrate on, other things to worry about besides where he was going to live.

His footsteps slowed as he approached the stone bungalow on Maple. With a sense of shock, he noticed that the *for sale* sign had been removed, and another sign hung from the rails on the front porch.

A deep sense of sadness overwhelmed him as he realized he'd been too late. He'd let his insecurities and annoying sense of what was right cloud his desire to have that house.

Oh, well. It figured the house would sell the day he finally decided to talk to Dinah about it.

This was typical of the kind of day he was having. Hopefully his talk with Dinah later in the day would turn his luck around, and she'd forgive him. Really, if he was honest with himself, the house meant nothing without her and Bryan to share it with.

It was amazing that the new owner had managed to have the electricity turned on, and even had a mat near the front porch. He glanced at the sign. "Welcome Home, Jeremy."

He came to a dead stop and looked up.

There, peeking out the window, stood a beaming Dinah, Bryan in her arms. "Hey, soldier," she called out. "Care to come in for a spell?"

He couldn't believe his eyes. Striding up the steps, he glanced at everything in confusion. "Dinah?"

She came out on the front porch to meet him, a wide smile playing on her lips. "Hey."

He brushed his fingers along Bryan's soft hair, then gazed into her eyes. "What's going on?"

She set Bryan on the floor, next to a basket of his favorite bowls and spoons. "After you left, I spoke with Mrs. McKinley."

"Marianne?"

She nodded. "All I could think about was my harsh words driving you away," she said, her tone serious. "I couldn't bear it."

Feeling shameful he countered, "It wasn't you . . . I said those things and left without even letting you explain yourself, or telling you something, too."

She pointed to the front stoop. "Can I tell you now?"

He nodded, and sat beside her.

"I was so worried about loving again. About getting hurt again," she said admitted quietly. "I let myself focus on things that didn't matter, like our age differences, or how other people might think of us being together . . . instead of what was in my heart."

His blue-gray eyes glowed. "What is in your heart?"

"Happiness," she said with a smile. "Love for you." How happy I am with you."

"I've let myself worry about silly things too," he admitted. "I worried that you wouldn't want me unless I could provide for you like Neil did."

She clasped his hand. "I only wanted you, not another Neil." She sighed. "After hearing you talk about your love for me, how you were willing to do so much to make me feel loved, I realized that your motives were from your heart. Just because I don't need you to provide for me financially doesn't mean I don't need you. I do need you, in all the ways you said. I do love you, Jeremy."

He held her close, then laughed as she wrinkled her nose when she came in contact with the wet wool. "Help me get this off, would you?"

"With pleasure."

She easily complied, and the freedom Jeremy felt clad only in a T-shirt lifted his spirits. That, and Dinah's wonderful words. "I love you. That's why I want to marry you. I should have told you that first off. I should have told you that weeks ago."

Her pretty brown eyes softened. "I love you, too . . . and . . . I want to marry you, too."

His heart slammed into his chest. Forcing himself

to breath deep and not rush things, he gestured to the house. "What happened here?"

"Well, I started thinking that I love this house, too," she said, her dimple appearing. "I have actually walked by here often, thinking about how cozy and interesting it felt."

"So you bought it?" He tried to feel excited, but he couldn't shake the fact that she accomplished something so easily which had been almost impossible for him to obtain.

She shook her head. "No."

Now he was thoroughly confused. "No? Then how . . . why are you here?"

"I paid half of it. Marianne said that my half, combined with your half of the earnest money, would be more than enough. She called the owner's agent right then and there."

"And he said okay, that quickly?"

She nodded. "Yep. He really doesn't want this place. And it's not ours officially yet, it will probably take a few weeks to do everything up right. But Marianne said it would be all right if I sat in here and waited for you to come by."

"And put up a sign."

"Yes. And put up a sign," she said softly.

"How did you know I'd be passing this way?"

"I called your family and asked them to please help me out." She gestured to her cell phone. "You've practically been tailed the whole way here."

He laughed. "This . . . this is the most amazing thing anyone's ever done for me. Thank you."

He pulled her into his arms and kissed her over and over, until each felt as if their limbs were made of noodles. Bryan soon got into the action, and crawled up into Jeremy's lap, demanding his own set of kisses.

Finally, when they pulled apart, Jeremy scooted down two steps, so he was well and truly kneeling in front of her. "Dinah, will you and Bryan marry me? Will you make me the happiest man in Payton?"

She smiled brightly, gifting him with a bright display of twin dimples. "Jeremy Reece, I'd be honored."

With a yell of pleasure, he grasped her hands, kissed her knuckles, then opened his arms for Bryan's embrace.

"This is how it's supposed to be, isn't it?" Dinah asked after they kissed again.

"What?"

"Being so happy . . . finding love with you. Isn't it something, the two of us . . . finding love, right here in Payton?"

It was something. And pretty wonderful.

Her words couldn't have been more true.